SUPERIOR DILEMMA

A Lake Superior Mystery

Other books by Matthew Williams

The Lake Superior Mystery Series:
Superior Death
Superior Deception

SUPERIOR
DILEMMA

•

Matthew Williams

AVALON BOOKS
NEW YORK

Published by Avalon Books,
an imprint of Thomas Bouregy & Co., Inc.
160 Madison Avenue, New York, NY 10016

Library of Congress Cataloging-in-Publication Data

Williams, Matthew, 1963–
    Superior dilemma : a Lake Superior mystery / Matthew Williams.
        p.   cm.
    ISBN 978-0-8034-7674-5 (alk. paper)
1. Superior, Lake, Region—Fiction.   2. City and town life—
Michigan—Fiction.   3. Journalists—Michigan—Fiction.
I. Title.
    PS3623.I55868S87 2011
    813'.6—dc22

                                                    2011005605

PRINTED IN THE UNITED STATES OF AMERICA
ON ACID-FREE PAPER
BY RR DONNELLEY, BLOOMSBURG, PENNSYLVANIA

This book is dedicated to Suzanne and Sam "The Frog." They keep me on an even keel during the worst of storms.

Acknowledgments

I am grateful to Jackie and Jim Winkowski of Snowy Plains Kennel for answering my questions about sled dogs, and also to Chief L. "Mike" Angeli of the Marquette City Police and Assistant U.S. Attorney Maarten Vermaat for steering me straight on a few procedural questions. On behalf of all writers, I'd also like to thank the real Erin Donovan, who works to ensure that the next generation's readers develop a love of literature.

Chapter One

Trust me: there is no worse place to lose your toddler than at the start of the Superior Sled Dog Challenge—our frigid, northern version of Rio Carnivale. I had lowered my three-year-old off my shoulders for only a moment, long enough to adjust the hat she'd shoved over my eyes, when she scooted into the boot-stomping, parka-clad, partying horde that packs our downtown each February.

I called, but even if my headstrong daughter was inclined to listen, she'd never hear me above the music, the cheering, or the amped-up emcee who was trying to out-howl three-hundred-plus canines. The dogs, straining against their leads, were eager to escape the pageantry and start their journey: two hundred and fifty miles on silent, winding trails through Northern Michigan wilderness.

Hoping to catch sight of her pink parka, I pried my way through the crowd, stepping on toes and catching elbows in the ribs.

"Watch it!" a guy shouted and shoved back. His frosty beer breath rose against fine snowflakes. Our weather guru had predicted at least a foot would fall tonight.

"I'm looking for a little girl!" I shouted. The crowd's roar drowned me out. I was already off the man's radar as the next twelve-dog team shot past.

The voice of Jack Reynolds bellowed from massive speakers. Musher twenty-three, Earl someone, hailing from someplace like Mosquito Junction, Minnesota, had headed off into the night.

Every year our city closes Main Street on the first Friday in February. City crews haul back the snow they've worked so hard to remove and Apostle Bay throws a huge party kicking off our Midwestern version of the Iditarod.

The dogs, torqued by the glitz and pandemonium, and desperate to run by breeding and training, sprint east out of town. They fly down a hill to Lake Superior and then head south along an abandoned railroad grade that follows the shoreline. Mushers carry extra weight at the race start and ride hard on their snow brake just to slow their teams and get the dogs running at an even pace.

Last year, on assignment, I'd been one team's deadweight. After seeing this circus from inside the orange snow fence, I learned why mushers from around the country keep coming back to Apostle Bay—why there's a waiting list of entrants. It's not the chance to win the solid gold Superior Cup worth twenty-five grand that draws them; rather, it's the few minutes we make rock stars out of lonely men and women who spend the bulk of their lives on isolated backwoods trails.

I shouted and shoved against the pulsing mob, starting toward each flash of pink until I was spun in futile circles. Despair drove me back out of the crowd and toward the elevated stage near the starting line. If anyone could get the crowd's attention and find my little baby it'd be Jack with his microphone. In a small corner of my mind I just hoped my wife Deb, tucked away in a little diner nearby, didn't hear his announcement.

Deb had wanted a quiet night at home. I'd insisted we join the festivities. This was the first year since we'd moved to Apostle Bay that I could kick back and spectate rather than work the race as a reporter. Besides, I thought the fresh air would be great for Deb. She's stressing over a new class she teaches at Bay High, a situation made worse by the town's old-timers who keep complaining to the school board that she's perpetrating some form of hippie brainwashing.

It's a civics course, a break from her normal science curriculum, and it sounded right up her alley: to get the students involved in local political issues. They take a current event, study the pros and cons, and then make a presentation to the City Commission. Instead of having half our town outraged, a role I think Deb once took pleasure in as a community activist, she now has everyone ticked off.

I'd told her to steer clear of topics close to the population's heart, such as snowmobile rights. But she forgets it's a different world north of the forty-fifth parallel, where the sun rarely appears in winter and we average fifteen feet of annual snowfall.

This evening, soon after we'd arrived to watch the race, a crank with a grizzled beard and a blaze orange knit cap got in her face, blaming her for the recent spate of vandalism to local snowmobile trails—as if Deb were personally dragging logs over the track and removing signs. I told him to get a life, but that, along with the crowd noise and claustrophobic atmosphere, had ruined her evening.

I'd left Deb in the back corner of the Laughing Whitefish Café with my mother, a cup of herbal tea, and the promise that Glory and I would watch a few teams start and then we'd cruise home. Instead, I was experiencing a panic attack, and my independent little buckaroo was gone.

Ten yards from the stage I shouted for Jack's attention.

"Whoa, there!" he blared into the mic, oblivious to me. "Someone grab those dogs."

I followed his gaze and saw chaos spreading through the start area. Dogs bounded free, some running in circles, some howling and chasing after the last team down the starting chute. Volunteers grasped at dog harnesses. A musher in a blue-hooded parka, his headlamp bobbing as she shouted, restrained two dogs with one hand and pointed a bare finger at a third. In front of her, exposed to claws, teeth, and swinging ganglines, stood my Glory.

I veered from the stage and screamed for someone to grab my little girl. Jack, instead of directing people to help, was making noise about parents needing to keep track of their children. My co-worker Gina Holt, the reporter covering this event, was the closest adult with a free hand, but she stood frozen in place, with an expression I'd never seen on her face: fear.

"Gina, grab Glory!"

A white dog with streaks of brown, short-haired, lean, its muzzle the height of my daughter's neck, locked blue eyes on Glory. I shouted for Gina again. Glory stepped toward the dog.

"Grab her harness!" the musher yelled. "Morning Glory, stay!"

My daughter's nickname?

I shoved people aside, closing the gap.

"Bella, grab her!" the musher screamed.

A handler in brown canvas overalls, already restraining one animal, reached for the dog. I shouldered the last person between me and the melee, intent on diving in front of my little girl, when a mountainous brown coat blocked my way.

Ben Bowerman snagged Glory, swung her up onto his shoulders, and turned toward me. I was still crouched for my leap.

"Missing something?"

"Oh, thank God, Ben," I said, straightening and touching Glory's leg to reassure myself. There was no safer place than atop the shoulders of Doctor Ben, as my daughter called him. The emergency room physician towers over most people. He's solid and rough as the exposed granite in our woods. He's also the Superior Challenge race director.

"Glory, what were you doing over there?" I interjected. Expecting tears in her eyes, I saw only a twinkle of excitement.

"She obviously thought they were calling her," Ben said. His tone was clear: I'd screwed up, not my toddler.

"That's Lupine Ryder's team," he said. "Her dogs broke loose back in the staging area. Ryder and her handler were calling them: Hyacinth, Buttercup, Morning Glory . . . Get it now? Glory must have heard her pet name."

He nodded toward the blue-clad musher. She was ripping her handler a new one, to the obvious embarrassment of the volunteers holding her other dogs.

Gina, I noticed, still hadn't moved, hadn't even raised her camera to snap photos.

Another musher, with volunteers straining to hold his dogs in check, moved past and into the starting chute. Jack explained something about a time adjustment over the PA system.

"She names her dogs after flowers?" I said.

"Poisonous flowers," Ben replied. "Nightshade Kennels. It fits her personality."

Jack began a countdown for the next team. The crowd joined him, and if Ben said more, it was drowned out by the ensuing roar. Cowbells clanged. The sled leaped forward.

I watched the team grow distant, thinking that the cowbells had taken on a different tone. Then I realized people weren't looking down the chute anymore; they'd turned around toward the storefronts. An alarm of some kind was ringing.

"It's Iverson's Gold Rush," Ben said, able to see over everyone's heads. "Either someone's robbed Perry, or his store's on fire."

Chapter Two

The alarm cut off and for a brief moment downtown echoed with only the animal sounds of yipping and howling. Jack broke the spell. "Looks like someone rang Perry Iverson's bell."

The crowd whooped and hollered.

"Hey, let's join the Gold Rush and ring these puppies forward!" Jack shouted. "C'mon people, give it up for Lu-u-u-u-pine Ryder."

The din returned and the musher with dogs named after toxic flowers edged into the chute.

"What's going on?" I asked Ben.

"Keep a tighter rein on her, Vince," Ben said, swinging my daughter off his shoulders and onto mine, a move that packed snow down my neck. "I'm going to find out."

I glanced toward the start line looking again for Gina. She's been a news reporter for more than a year now, promoted from editorial assistant and obit writer after our last hire crashed and burned. She was probably working her way toward Perry's to find out what happened. I decided to fall in behind Ben, just in case she was delayed.

Glory squirmed and kicked.

"My doggies."

"Sorry, girl. You'll get to see the doggies again soon."

She twisted, grunted, yanked my hat over my eyes, and battled me all the way to Iverson's Gold Rush, a family-owned jewelry shop that's been here longer than paved streets. Stuffed toy huskies in the window display saved me from a full-blown tantrum.

"Pretty doggies," she said.

The toy dogs, along with glitter, fake snow, a single weathered snowshoe, and a mushing harness, lay on a worn red velvet display. Centered on a pedestal, lit by two overhead halogen lamps, was an eighteen-inch replica of the Superior Cup.

The real cup is solid gold and much smaller, like something out of a cereal box. People not close to the sport probably wonder why a musher would suffer through three lonely, sleepless, frigid days and nights for a chance to win it.

The grand prize is sponsored by the Elk Ridge Hunt and Fish Club, the exclusive establishment for the wealthy that is an hour north of Apostle Bay. Race organizers say under their breath that they'd rather have a check or a pile of cash for the mushers instead of a solid gold cup. But the club is big on tradition and also on getting its own way.

So each year Perry Iverson makes the trophy—its size depends on the current price of gold. Then, if rumor is true, he'll buy it back on Monday morning after the awards ceremony, paying seventy-five cents on the dollar. The mushers then buy dog food and replace worn harnesses. Perry uses the gold for his custom-made wedding bands and other jewelry he sells during the year.

We approached a barrel-chested patrolman who blocked the entrance to Perry's store. He turned away a few gawkers who wanted a peek inside.

"What's happened?" Ben asked. "Perry's soldering iron set off the fire alarm or something?"

The patrolman answered: "Robbery. Perry pulled the fire alarm and the thief escaped out the back. Chief Weathers is inside. He said if I saw you I should send you in."

"Is someone hurt?"

"No. Something to do with the race—you're in charge of that, right?"

"Sometimes I wonder." Ben sighed.

The patrolman pushed open the door. I tried to follow.

"Sorry, just Ben."

"I'm with him," I said.

Ben looked back to us, lifted a single eyebrow, and then shrugged. "They're with me."

"The chief said nobody but you and Detective Greenleaf."

"We might need his help," Ben said, nodding at me.

"But—"

"I'll take the heat if Dale disagrees."

Police chief Dale "Ramrod" Weathers, my godfather, would not only disagree, he'd hand this poor patrolman his head before the night was out. That didn't stop me from following Ben.

When the door swung closed, Ben said, "I only did that because I know you'd just go straight around the block and try to sneak in the back door with Glory. Don't make me regret it. Play with the stuffed huskies or something while I see what Dale wants."

"Ben, c'mon, I just wanted to get Glory out of the cold."

He snorted and went to the shop's back room where we heard voices behind heavy maroon drapes.

The Gold Rush showroom is small. Glass display cases line the two side walls. A semicircular pedestal case stands in the room's center. The drapes covered the view of Perry's workshop.

Part of the store's attraction, maybe the only attraction considering the sparse stock on display, was watching Perry work his craft. It was a tourist thing, I guess.

I lowered Glory. She made a beeline for the sled dog display, snagged a stuffed husky and, before I could reach her, climbed onto the pedestal to nab the other.

"Glory, get down from there," I hissed.

I lifted her clear, relieved she hadn't destroyed anything. She settled on the floor with the two dogs.

I drifted toward the voices while trying to watch her with one eye.

"Calm down, Perry," I heard the chief say. "Now explain this to me again."

"They stole the cup. It's gone." Perry's voice squeaked out the last two words. A nervous, twitchy person any time he wasn't absorbed in his work, Perry was likely fidgeting to distraction under the chief's gaze.

"They?" the chief asked.

"He, I mean, she . . . I don't know. The person wore a mask."

"Just one person?"

"Yeah. He had a gun, so I gave him the cup."

"So it was a man? Can you describe him?"

"Yes. No. I mean, I don't know. It might have been a woman. I wasn't . . . You know, the person was small . . . They wore a mask, and it all happened so fast."

"Calm down, Perry," the chief said, although his voice sounded far from soothing, more like he was annoyed that Perry couldn't remember details.

"Ben, I've got a feeling your musher Earl Parsons is part of this," the chief said.

"He's not *my* musher."

"I've called in the officers who were out patrolling the snow-mobile trails and we'll send a car to the first road crossing. In the meantime, can you get the ham radio guys to track him?"

The storefront door opened and I turned to find my friend,

detective captain Gordon Greenleaf, bundled in a navy parka and jeans. He stomped the snow off his boots and shook his head when he saw me.

"Vince, what are you doing here?"

"Shopping for a Valentine's Day gift."

Glory ran across the room to him. "Look what I got, Gord."

Gord stooped down to her level and studied the stuffed toys she held forward.

"What's going on in here?" the chief roared.

My red-faced godfather held the curtain open. Behind him, I saw Perry wringing his hands and pacing.

"Chief," Glory shouted. She ran to him with the huskies.

"Good grief, Vince. What are you doing here? No, don't answer that. Just go."

"But, Chief," I said, "we needed a place to get warm."

"Yeah, and I hear the *Chronicle*'s got doughnuts and coffee."

"Did someone really steal the Superior Cup?" I asked.

Perry bobbed his head.

"Look, Chief," Glory said, holding the dogs toward him.

"Yeah, honey. I'm kind of busy now. Take your papa back outside."

"Who's Earl Parsons?" I asked. "The name sounds familiar."

"If you're not out that door in three seconds, I'll embarrass you in front of your daughter, and you don't want that, *capice?*"

"But why do you—"

"One," he said.

"Yeah, okay. C'mon, sweetheart. Put the doggies back and let's go find Mama."

"No," she said.

"Glory, they're not yours."

She twisted away.

"Let her keep them," the chief said.

"But—"

"Scram."

I snagged Glory and swung her up into my arms, ignoring the glint of triumph in her smile. As we passed Gordon, I whispered, "I'll call."

"I won't answer."

We stepped back out into the street as the cowbells sent another musher off into the night. Reynolds exhorted the crowd to give a shout-out to some team from Ontario. And my managing editor's ringtone sounded in my chest pocket.

Chapter Three

It's Lou-oo," my daughter said, mimicking her mom's sarcastic tone.

We steered wide of the crowd and started toward the Laughing Whitefish Café, a throwback greasy diner that's easily the most popular joint in Apostle Bay.

"Go ahead, you can't help yourself," Glory said, again echoing her mother.

"Watch me."

This was supposed to be our family night together and I'd already ditched Deb for part of it. Between my wife's after-school obligations, my crazy work hours, and our toddler who rarely seems to sleep, Deb and I don't see enough of each other.

These days I work the early-morning shift, go home at midday to care for Glory, and then head back out in the evenings to cover the news desk or government meetings after Deb gets home. The schedule is great for child care, but horrible on family time.

Since Gina never turned up at Perry's store, Lou most likely wanted me to find out what had happened. He'd have to wait until morning.

At the café I lowered Glory, pulled the door open, and took in the aroma of meatloaf and mashed potatoes. Normally a place of clattering dishes and conversation, there was a temporary lull in the diner tonight. Most customers were outside cheering for the dogs. When the last musher tooled out of town later

12

this evening, the waitresses would be pouring hot chocolate and slinging pie to a standing-room-only crowd.

Seeing my mom, Loretta, and Deb in a back booth, my social butterfly offered a quick greeting to the waitress behind the counter and ran ahead.

"Look at this," she squealed, waving the stuffed toys over her head.

"Cool," Mom said. She stepped from the booth, scooped Glory into a powerful hug, and swung her in a circle, showing energy women twenty years her junior couldn't muster.

They settled into the vinyl seat opposite Deb, who offered a tired smile. My wife's eyes, normally deep pools of brown mirth just like her daughter's, seemed dull tonight. I bent down, kissed her forehead, and then pulled a chair over from the table behind me.

Lou paged me again. I unzipped my coat and silenced the phone.

"Aren't you going to answer it?" Deb asked.

"Nah," I said. "He has Gina, Mort, and Dr. Death on tonight. They can survive without me. Let's head home before the crowd descends on this place."

"Where'd you get the toys?" Mom asked Glory.

"At the store," she said.

"Iverson's Gold Rush," I added. "It's a long story. And my little Morning Glory"—I aimed my stern gaze at her—"we have to return them tomorrow."

Glory shot me the not-in-your-lifetime look and spun toward Mom.

"You should call Lou back," Deb said. "Gina went home sick. He sounded kind of desperate."

"Huh?"

"Lou called me a few minutes ago. Gina has the flu or something."

"I saw Gina at the start, and . . . Hey, how'd he get your cell number?"

Deb shrugged. Mom pretended she wasn't listening.

"Deb, I'm taking the night off. So let's cruise before he calls the diner or, worse yet, sends someone down here to find me."

"Vince, I'm really not feeling all that well."

"Because of that jerk earlier tonight? Don't let—"

"It's not that. I'm just really tired. And my back hurts. I probably strained something. All I want to do is go home and crash."

"I'm up for that," I said. I stood and reached a hand toward her.

Deb's phone rang in her purse. She pulled it out and handed it to me.

"Go on, Vince, really; it's fine. Loretta said she'll take us home. I won't be good company."

I looked from my mom to Deb and back. Mom shrugged. The phone kept chirping, so I silenced it and handed it back to Deb.

"Is this one of those marriage tests?" I asked. "Where you say one thing but really mean the opposite?"

When that comment didn't elicit a dirty look, I knew for sure my wife wasn't feeling well. She gathered her gloves and hat and started from the booth.

"Go on," she said. "I'd rather have a night together when I'm feeling better. Think of this as a rain check. Lou will owe you one."

Chapter Four

I sat in the booth a few moments after they'd left, wondering what I'd missed. That was *so* not Deb. Whatever had happened, Mom would clue me in later with a figurative slap upside the head.

I called the *Chronicle*.

"About time," Lou growled.

"I'm already on it, Lou. It's armed robbery. A gunman stole the Superior Cup from Iverson's. The cops suspect a musher named Parsons."

I heard papers riffling and keyboards clacking in the background.

"Lou, you there?"

"Armed robbery?"

"Yes."

"You have art?"

"I'm not working tonight, remember?"

"What's that got to do with anything? You keep a camera in your car."

"Yeah, and that's where it was when the burglary happened."

"I see." A year ago he would have blistered me with a two-minute diatribe about my failure to produce. These days he was taking baby steps toward mellowness with herbal tea and yogic meditation as the result of a budding romance with our local historian—or fear of a second heart attack. Life around the office was becoming bearable.

"What happened to Gina?"

"She let us down, stomach flu or food poisoning or some excuse. I . . . Ah, here it is: Earl Parsons, from Burning Pines, Minnesota, bib twenty-three. Hold it . . . Mort said a call went out to watch for this guy."

Our city beat reporter, Mort Maki, is also an amateur radio hack. The one event he enjoys covering each year, the only time a little color seems to brighten his pasty skin, is the Sled Dog Challenge. He brings in his equipment, sets up a command center, talks in code names, guzzles two-liter bottles of Dew, and covers the entire three-day race without sleep.

"The ham operators are tracking him," I said. "The cops hope to catch him at one of the road crossings, or at the Dahinda checkpoint, although I don't expect he'll stay on course if he's guilty."

"Why are they keying on Parsons?" Lou asked.

"The chief seems certain that Parsons is the guy. The name rings familiar, but I can't place it."

"Mort said that too. We'll look into it. In the meantime, get me some art and— Not now Holmes, I— Huh. . . ."

I heard Thomas Holmes, our new obit writer, telling Lou something. The staff refers to Holmes as Dr. Death, and he seems to enjoy the moniker. A retired funeral home director—he prefers mortuary scientist—who has a penchant for flowery prose, Holmes is our new obit writer. His copy drives Lou bonkers, but families of the recently dead love his work. And they pay by the column inch, so he's boosted revenue.

Behind me the café's door jingled and a group of revelers pushed their way inside, stomping their feet, yanking off gloves, and brushing snow off their shoulders. Outside the café's window a curtain of fine, powdery snow obscured my view of the harbor.

Lou growled a few expletives and then came back on the line.

"Vince, I want you at the Dahinda checkpoint when they catch this guy. Holmes tells me Parsons is originally from Apostle Bay."

"So?"

"Apparently he robbed a bank and killed his wife before he left town the last time."

Now I knew why the name was familiar, and why Gina had called in sick. Earl Parsons was her son-in-law.

Chapter Five

I recall little about the bank heist or the murder. A self-absorbed teen at the time, my news cycle was limited to gossip among parents and my classmates. And my peers moved on to juicier, more hormonal stuff after a day or two of anything.

I realize now it must have circulated for some time through the adult circles, because murder is so rare in Apostle Bay and unsolved murder even less common. I also don't think we'd had a successful bank robbery since John Dillinger swung through the Upper Peninsula in the 1930s. We're a town that tends toward simple crimes, and because everyone knows everyone else, it's hard to get away with much.

Witnesses swore Earl Parsons robbed the bank. However, he could prove he was on the other side of the county when the crime went down. And the cops never found his wife's body. Gina, I seem to recall, was estranged from her daughter at the time. That's about the extent of my knowledge.

I dialed Gina's cell phone to see if she would share more, but got her voice mail. The first mushers would arrive at the Dahinda checkpoint in about two hours. I could beat them there if the roads were decent, which shows how things have changed in the last hundred and fifty years.

When the trapper John Marbury—one of our town's twelve founders or "apostles"—made the original dogsled trip that the Challenge is based upon, it took his team a full day to reach Dahinda. Of course, he didn't have dogs bred for racing, nor groomed trails.

Marbury had gone after the schooner *Blazing Comet* during the harsh winter of 1849. The ship, with the town's winter supplies, was locked in the ice of Potlach Bay, a hundred miles west. Marbury led three teams through a blizzard to the bay. They commandeered the ship at gunpoint when the captain refused to sail her due to the weather, hired Native Americans to chop a path through the ice to open water, and then sailed the supplies to Apostle Bay and a hero's welcome.

The recent discovery of Marbury's other deeds has since tarnished his reputation, though his fortitude that winter undeniably saved Apostle Bay's first settlement.

I cut through the alley a block south of Main Street and turned toward the *Chronicle*'s employee parking lot where I'd left my Bronco. Wheels spinning on slick pavement caught my attention, and I looked up to see Gina's sky blue pickup fishtail out of the lot and speed off. She hadn't looked sick at the start line, just stunned, but that didn't make sense. She's been covering the race for a few days now and had to know about Earl's return. She had probably even run across him at a musher event. I tried her cell again with no luck.

Moments later I was headed south and west out of the city, the snow flying into my high beams like a jump to hyperspace. I passed a couple of mushers' pickup trucks with wooden dog boxes in the bed and spare wicker sleds tied on top. They too were racing to Dahinda.

I called Mom.

"Where are you now?" she asked.

"Heading to Dahinda. How's Deb?"

"Not feeling well. She's waiting out in the car. We stopped at my place for a few things. I'll stay with her until you get home."

"You think I should turn back?"

"Deb said if you called I'm supposed to tell you no." Her tone told me she didn't agree.

"Keep me posted, okay?"

"Sure."

Off to my left, through the snow, I saw a tiny bright spot, like a fairy light, bobbing along the lakeshore. It was a musher's headlamp. The teams follow the old railroad grade south, before turning west under a bridge and cutting cross-country on forest service and seasonal roads for a while. In another few miles I'd turn west too, and I wouldn't see mushers again until Dahinda. It would be hard for the cops to find anyone through that stretch.

"I need you to refresh my memory about Earl Parsons," I continued, "the guy who robbed the bank and bumped off his wife about, what, thirteen, fourteen years ago."

"He's not the same Earl Parsons, is he?" said Mom. "When I saw the name on the start list, I figured it was just a coincidence."

"It's not."

"That explains things," she said.

"What things?"

"Like why Dale's been distracted."

Although they've been a couple for more than a year now, it still sounds weird hearing Mom call Dale by his name instead of referring to him as "the chief" like she'd done since I was a toddler.

"He didn't say anything to you about Parsons?" I asked.

"Are you serious?"

"Sorry, I know it's not his style. Anyway, I remember it was fall during football season; beyond that the details are fuzzy."

"The story is that Earl walked into the bank wearing a ski mask, pulled a gun on the teller, and got away with five thousand, maybe eight thousand dollars, something like that. People saw his truck. It was easy to recognize because it had the dog boxes. Oh, and he hit another car when he was driving away. I think people inside the bank recognized him too, even with the mask. And there was something about a bullet; he fired a gun into the bank ceiling and the bullet matched his gun, or something."

"But he had an alibi, right? He was helping someone across the county at the same time?"

"Some tourists," she said. "Earl was out running his dogs with the four-wheeler and came across these fall color tourists whose car was stuck in a ditch. He helped them get it out.

"I remember Dale's frustration," she continued. "He couldn't figure out how to get around that alibi—the tourist was a retired judge and he was absolutely sure of the time Earl helped him—just like witnesses were absolutely sure Earl was behind that ski mask."

"What about his wife?"

"She was in the truck, riding shotgun as he drove away, and that's the last time anyone saw her. The truck turned up a few days later, abandoned on some two-track."

"Why would Parsons return after all these years?"

"Maybe you should ask him," Mom said.

"I hope I get the chance to."

Chapter Six

I arrived at the Dahinda fairgrounds a little after ten. In the time it took to dig out my camera, pull on a hat and gloves, and gather a notebook, snow had already covered my windshield.

The Dahinda checkpoint is a far cry from the glitz of downtown Apostle Bay. Two sodium vapor lamps bathed the assortment of snow-covered trucks and SUVs with orange light. A few snowmobile engines whined in the distance. Voices drifted my way from a small group surrounding a bonfire.

I headed toward the checkpoint headquarters, a faded blue pole barn where 4-H kids displayed animals in the summer.

The Superior Challenge has three checkpoints: here, Potlach, and here again on the way back. Mushers choose where to rest their teams, and most take only a brief food and water stop here. They prefer running through the night while the temperature is better for the dogs and the team is still fresh.

At the race's midpoint, another seventy-five miles west in Potlach, the dogs have a mandatory vet check and the officials inspect the racer's sled bags. All competitors are required to carry safety equipment and provisions on the journey. Bag checks at midpoint and at the finish ensure they don't ditch the stuff midcourse so the dogs have less weight to pull.

I rounded the barn and planned to step inside when someone shouted that the first team was arriving. Spectators rang their cowbells and whooped. A race official in an orange vest lumbered toward the flag stretched between two poles labeled CHECKPOINT. Beyond the hay bale chute, a point of bluish light glowed. Then I saw Gord cut across the snow toward the race official.

I changed direction as the dogs came into view at the fairground's far edge. The sled split a seam in the fresh snow. Powder covered the sled bag and musher.

"Bib sixteen," someone called.

The musher leaned back, his full weight on the snow brake as they neared the chute. He guided his team between the pipes. I snapped photos of the team's handler grabbing the gangline at the lead dog. Two volunteers snagged the line further back. They trotted the team toward a silver pickup where the musher set his snow hook and I followed, hoping to get art for tomorrow's edition.

The race official asked about the trail conditions. The musher looked up into the falling snow first, finally giving me a decent view of his face to photograph, and then said, "At least there's no wind."

"Yet," the official said. "It's supposed to pick up by midnight."

Comfortable that I had enough to satisfy Lou, I tucked my camera inside my coat and found Gord, still hanging near the chute. He shook his head when he saw me coming.

"Why don't you turn your cell phone on?" I said.

"Why don't you quit calling when you know I won't answer?" he asked.

"Not in my nature. Since you're here, does that mean the state cops didn't pick Parsons off at a road crossing?"

"Pick him off?" he said, arching an eyebrow. "We're not playing a video game."

"You know what I mean."

"Here's another sled," someone shouted.

"Think this is our guy?" I asked.

"Now he's *our guy?*"

"Man, you're cynical tonight," I said.

Spectators converged on the chute and we all leaned forward. A couple of handlers moved in, waiting to see if it was their team.

"Bib seventeen," shouted someone with better eyesight than me. "It's Teej."

T. J. Donovan—Teej to most—is a local musher, a fan favorite, and the reigning Red Lantern winner. Like the red light on a train's caboose, the Red Lantern goes to the musher who finishes last. It's not that Teej has slow dogs, he just gets distracted. He stops along the way to chat with people, or to share a mug of cocoa and a bratwurst.

Teej's team came through the chute and I snapped a few photos of the huge, ever-present grin shining through his ice-laden beard. His wife and handler, Erin, grabbed the lead dog, nuzzled its head, and then walked the line touching each of the dogs in turn. Teej laughed his booming laugh, talked to volunteers, and generally socialized with the small crowd.

Meanwhile Erin worked back up the line and snagged the lead dog's harness. With help from a couple of race volunteers, she guided the team toward their truck. Teej slapped the race official on the back and started into some story about a moose he'd seen.

"A little help here, Teej," Erin called back.

"Yep, right on it," he said. Teej trotted after them, stopping every few steps to shake a gloved hand or nod a greeting.

I moved to Gord's side.

"If I stole the gold cup," I said, "I'd head in the opposite direction and wouldn't stop until I was deep into Canada."

"He's coming," Gord said. "There's his handler."

He nodded toward a rust-bucket brown pickup with the typical plywood kennels on the back and spare sled riding atop. A guy wearing faded Carhartts paced near the vehicle.

I watched him push a sleeve back, glance at his watch, and then look up the trail.

"He made it through the last road crossing about two minutes ahead of the state police," Gord added. "He's going to show."

"Then maybe he didn't steal anything," I said.

Gord shrugged. "I guess we'll find out soon enough."

To our left cowbells clanged. The musher who'd arrived first pulled up his snow hook and encouraged his dogs forward.

"What do you remember about the bank robbery?" I asked Gord.

"It happened during our senior season and, at the time, I was more worried about surviving Friday nights than local news stories."

"Yeah, that's my recollection too—you running for your life on the gridiron every week."

"No thanks to you," he said. "Watching my back from the bench."

"Hey, I was injured."

"Broke your leg running to the water jug?" He smiled. "Way to sacrifice yourself for the team."

"Better than getting stomped into the mud by a bunch of Neanderthals twice my size."

"Yeah, the good ol' days," Gord said.

I bounced on my toes to get the blood flowing again. A few more sled dog trucks were pulling in. The crowd around the bonfire had grown.

"Why did Parsons come back to Apostle Bay?" I asked.

Gord shrugged. "I stopped trying to understand people," he said. "It gets me nowhere."

"Incoming musher," someone shouted.

Spectators moved toward the chute again. I brushed the snow from my coat and pulled out the camera. If Teej was bib seventeen, then Parsons left twelve minutes behind him. He ought to be here any time now.

Gord put a foot up on the hay bale and seemed relaxed, but he wasn't looking down the trail. I followed his gaze over to Parsons' handler, who now grabbed a five-gallon bucket off the ground. He must have recognized something about the head-lamp or perhaps the sound of the dogs, because he started la-dling sled dog protein soup into dented bowls.

"Bib twenty-three," the official said.

"Stay out of the way," Gord said.

I leaped the hay bale and crossed the chute so I could get pho-tos of Gord interacting with Parsons when he arrived. I found Parsons' dogs through the lens and snapped off a few shots.

It may have been my camera perspective, but the dogs seemed to be moving much faster than the previous teams, almost like they were out of control. I stepped up onto a hay bale and glanced back at Parsons' truck, hoping to see what his handler was doing now.

"Get off there," the race official yelled.

I ignored him. The driver's door to Parsons' truck stood open and he was doing something at the steering wheel. Starting the engine? Grabbing a gun from the console? I checked Gord to see if he noticed and instead saw the Carhartt-clad handler pushing to the front of the crowd, getting ready to receive the dogs when they entered the chute.

I tried looking back toward the truck to see who was there. A hand tugged my jacket, pulling me off the bale.

"I said get off there."

I regained balance as the dogs barreled through, but missed a good shot when Parsons almost tipped the sled as he rode under the checkpoint sign.

The handler called "whoa" and grabbed the lead dog's gang-line as they ran past. For a moment I thought they'd pull him off his feet, but he moved with them, leaning back at the same time to slow the team. Parsons stumbled off the sled, as if he didn't have his land legs yet. Snow matted his fur-edged parka and encased his orange goggles. A frost-covered polypropylene mask protected his face.

The crowd parted to let them through. I shoved my way backward and jogged around spectators, trying to get in place ahead of them.

No such luck. The handler was already feeding the dogs. He knelt and whispered to each one, though they seemed more intent on gulping down the food than listening. Parsons followed him from dog to dog, gesturing with his hands, arguing about something. Gord closed in on them from the left.

The handler patted the wheel dog, the one closest to the sled, and then stood. Parsons threw up his hands, kicked at the snow, and then stalked over to the truck. He rooted through the equipment in his truck's bed, grabbed a bag, and tossed it toward the handler, who was now checking ganglines. I noticed the cab was still open, and thought I saw movement on the truck's far side.

Gord moved in between Parsons and his dogs and I watched the guy shift from foot to foot, looking past Gord to his team. Gord approached him, hand held up, probably displaying his ID.

Behind him the handler bellowed, "Get away from the dogs!"

I sidestepped and watched the handler stare down two race volunteers, their orange bibs compressing down coats like corsets. He kept staring until the volunteers backed away, and then he reached down and zipped up the sled's carryall. He kicked aside two feed bowls.

Back at the truck, Parsons pulled his mittens off and slapped them against his leg. His gaze bounced from the chute, to the dogs, to Gord, never resting.

"Here comes a team!" someone shouted from the chute area.

The cowbells clanged to life again. I turned to see Gord extend his ID toward the musher.

"Get outta my way!" the handler shouted.

He grabbed the sled's handles and started pushing it forward. I noticed the snow hook was up and hanging on the sled.

"Hike! Hike!" he shouted, the sled dog version of giddyup used to spur dogs forward.

The dogs lunged. The handler was now pushing the sled with them. A race official stumbled back, falling on his rump.

The handler stepped onto a runner as the sled gained speed. He scooter-kicked, helping the dogs accelerate.

"Gord!" I yelled.

Gord stepped toward the sled, and then seemed to realize there was nothing he could do. He turned back toward the musher.

"Stop him!"

"I couldn't even if I wanted to," the man answered.

I snapped photos of their standoff.

The race official stood and dusted snow off his pants.

"There wasn't anything I could do," he told Gord.

"I know," Gord said. He keyed his radio as the dogs reached the fairground's far end and disappeared into the forest.

Chapter Seven

Gord finished using his radio and, with a nod of his head toward the parking lot, told Parsons to follow.

"But—" the musher said.

"Save your breath," Gord said. He looked at me. "Don't touch anything, Vince. Someone's coming to secure the truck."

They started across the fairground and the race official fell in behind them. When they were out of earshot, I moved closer to Parsons' truck. The driver's door was still open and snow already covered part of the seat and floor. I leaned in for a peek and quickly jerked my head back to fresh air. The cab reeked of fresh dog feces.

How can anyone drive a truck that smells like that?

I walked back to the truck's bed and studied the plywood kennel boxes. A dog whimpered at one, its black nose poking at the airhole. The poor thing must have been thoroughly confused.

A spare race sled rested atop the boxes, its fiberglass runners, wicker frame, and triangular gear bag all covered with snow.

I moved past the tailgate to the passenger side and almost flattened Gina Holt.

"What the—"

"Surprised?" she said. Her purple parka blended in with the night. She held blue mittens in one hand, a cigarette in the other.

"Yeah. What I mean . . . Jeez, Gina, why didn't you tell us?"

She took a hit on her cigarette and blew it out the right side of her mouth. "Tell you what?"

29

"About Parsons being back in town. And what's up with the cigarette? You quit smoking."

She took another drag and glared at me.

"I was just taking a hiatus."

She flipped the butt into the snow between us, pulled her mittens on, and started toward the parking lot. I fell into step beside her.

"They think Parsons stole the cup. That's why Gord nabbed him."

She laughed. "You think so?"

"I don't have a clue."

"Who do you think took off in that sled?"

"The handler. You think he took off once he knew Gordon was a cop?"

"*That* was Earl on the sled. Your cop friend took away Jon Bishop, his handler."

"But . . . are you sure?"

"Earl is my son-in-law."

"Then the handler, this Bishop guy, was driving the team?"

"Amazing how quick you catch on," she said.

"You have to tell Gord."

She glanced at me and then stepped up the pace. "I don't have to do anything."

"Hey, that was you poking around inside his truck earlier, wasn't it?"

"Oh, yeah," she said. "I left Earl a little present. Too bad he won't get it."

"Huh?"

"A dog crap seat warmer. I couldn't wait to see the look on his face when he got back in the cab. Too bad he made the switcheroo."

"I'm confused."

We passed the chute area and veered toward the parking lot.

"Shove off, Vince. I'm busy."

"Look, Gina, I can't imagine what this is like for you—"

"You're right. So don't bother trying."

She cut between snowmobiles parked at the edge of the lot and I fell in behind her.

"Fair enough, but you had the race's start list. You were at the bib draw. You already knew Earl Parsons was back in town. Why'd you wait until tonight to freak out? All you had to do was tell someone—"

"Freak out? Hardly. I was glad to see that Earl entered the race. I planned a few surprises for him along the way."

She stopped and surveyed the lot. I stepped in front of her.

"Are you serious?"

"Do I look like I'm kidding?"

"But he allegedly killed your daughter. I thought you'd be more angry about his return."

"She was a nasty, self-centered, conniving fool who married Earl for his dogs. I'm not happy she's dead, but she was clearly heading down that road, and nothing I could do back then would change her course. Besides, the key word there was *allegedly*."

"Gina, c'mon."

"Don't tell me to c'mon. With your perfect little daughter and perfect little wife, you don't have a clue."

Something caught her eye and I followed her gaze to a midnight blue Silverado king cab. The bug-shield on the hood said NIGHTSHADE KENNELS. It had an Ontario license plate.

Gina stepped toward the truck as it rolled forward, the tires squeaking in the new snow. I thought she was going to reach out and touch it.

The driver inched past us, apparently looking for a way into the musher's staging area. I recognized the handler who'd helped corral the loose sled dogs at the race's start.

Behind us, cowbells kicked in again. I turned to see three teams were neck-and-neck across the field, heading toward the checkpoint.

The driver saw them too. She stopped, swung open her door, and stood up on the driver's seat to look over the truck's roof.

"Lupine!" she shouted.

Gina started toward her. The crowd's volume grew. Amid cries of "Whoa," one musher's voice pierced the night, urging her dogs forward.

Out in the field, two teams backed off while the leading team passed through the chute on the edge of control, driving spectators back. The musher leaned hard on the brake, stopped the team, and tossed down a snow hook. She stepped off the sled, shouted something at a race official, yanked the clipboard from his hands, and signed in. He gestured with his arms, seeming to ask a question, but the musher returned to the sled and, without a glance toward the staging area, jerked the snow hook free.

"Wait, Lupine!" shouted the woman from the truck.

Ryder's team strained against their ganglines and she kicked the sled forward.

I squinted, trying to see her bib number and got blasted by the truck's horn. The driver was waving Gina away from the truck.

"Hold up!" Gina yelled.

The driver pulled forward. Gina ran alongside the cab.

"Wait a minute!" she yelled.

The pickup accelerated away from her. Gina changed direction, cutting between vehicles. I spotted her sky blue pickup two rows over and raced her to it.

Gina arrived a dozen steps ahead of me and yanked open the door. I caught her while she fumbled in her pockets for keys and grabbed her arm.

"What's going on?"

She yanked free, slid into the driver's seat, and then fired up the truck.

"Back away, Vince," she said, trying to pull her door closed. I held it open.

"Gina, what are you doing?"

"Get out of my way!"

"No, not until you tell—"

"You wanna know why I called in sick tonight? It has nothing to do with Earl's return. It's her," she said, pointing through the windshield toward the pickup's taillights disappearing down the road. "That driver. The one who's getting away right now."

"Why?"

"Because she's a dead ringer for Amy."

"Your daughter?"

"Yeah, *my daughter.* My daughter when she was a kid."

"It's just a coincidence."

"And she shows up here the same day Earl does? I don't think so."

"You're not thinking straight because of—"

She put the truck in reverse and forced me backward with the door. I stumbled and spun around. Once I cleared the door, Gina slammed it shut. Her wipers pushed a load of snow off the windshield, and then she spun her wheels and took off after the Nightshade girl.

Chapter Eight

I watched her truck disappear into the storm and then pulled out my cell to call Lou. I had two missed calls: Mom and the *Chronicle.*

I dialed work first. Holmes, aka Dr. Death, answered with his suave, funeral parlor demeanor.

"Good evening Vince. How goes the big—"

"Is Lou there?"

"He is, but he just stepped out to brew another cup of herbal tea. I think he's trying a vanilla flavor tonight."

"Then transfer me to Mort."

"I can do that, but before I do, I want to—"

"I'm kind of in a hurry here."

"Sure, sure. I'll send you over to him. But before I do—"

"C'mon, Holmes."

"Is that you, Vince?" Lou must have grabbed the phone out of Holmes' hand. I heard the man in the background telling Lou to pass on some message to me.

"Deadline's midnight," Lou said. "Maybe I can stretch it a little, so you've got two hours. Get to Potlach and file from there."

"Potlach? But I've got to find Gordon Greenleaf, tell him what's happening."

"What do you mean?" Lou growled. "Greenleaf's on his way to Potlach already."

"No, he's not. He's here. He thinks he's arrested Earl Parsons, but it's the wrong guy."

34

"Where have you been?" Lou said. "They've already figured it out."

I spun around, scanning the parking lot for Gord's sedan. I saw it at the far exit, turning out onto the road.

"But, how'd you—"

"The chief is here with Mort. They've got the radioheads working on it. I want you in Potlach."

"Lou, that's an hour and a half on a good night. The snow's really coming down."

"That's why you have four-wheel drive. Make sure you get me some art too. Oh, and tell your mother we're not her messenger service."

"What do you mean you're—"

I was talking to dead air.

Chapter Nine

From Dahinda, the race heads almost due west through rolling hills and frozen swampland to Potlach, a small fishing village on a protected Lake Superior bay. I knew from past years it would take the mushers at least two hours to cover the distance in decent conditions, but the new snow was going to make hard work for the teams.

The shortest way by car is a gravel U.S. Forest Service road. I pulled onto it and then flipped open my cell to check Mom's message. No signal, no surprise.

I put the phone in my cup holder and, with both hands on the wheel, kept it slow despite Lou's warning about the deadline. There wouldn't be any story if I ended up in the ditch.

Every once in a while, a handler's truck raced up behind me, leaned on the horn, and blew past, throwing up such a cloud of snow I'd have to slow to a crawl and wait for it to settle.

It was hard enough for me to follow tracks in the road. The mushers could easily miss a trail marker on a night like this, and since GPS units are banned by race rules, they'd be maneuvering by compass if they lost their way.

Two-thirds of the way through the desolate stretch, I came upon a line of SUVs and trucks parked near a left-side turnout. The vehicles squeezed the road down to a single lane. At the head of the turnout was a snow-covered sign. I'd arrived at the Lake Margaret public access—known more popularly as

Lake Margaritaville to a handful of people who came here to ice fish and party.

I'd stumbled upon this place last winter and written a story about their annual sled dog beach party. The mushers crossed the lake's northern edge here, not far from the road. Aristotle Thanatos, Apostle Bay's sexton, and his two sons had started the annual tradition of building a huge bonfire, setting up tents and spending two days and nights ice fishing, barbecuing, and cheering the mushers. Racers like Teej would stop and share a brew and a burger before returning to the trail.

The last vehicle in line, and the only one not covered by new snow, was a sky blue pickup, rammed deep into the bank.

I pulled in front of Gina's truck and created an orange disco effect on the falling snow with my hazard lights. From the way her tires had excavated grooves in the snow, it looked like Gina tried to spin herself free. I wiped her passenger window and looked inside the cab. No airbags deployed. The door was unlocked.

Thigh-deep footprints led away from the truck. Gina's probably, heading to the beach party in search of some brawny guys to push her out.

I called her name a few times as I walked along the road back toward the Lake Margaret sign. No answer. I turned and followed a snowmobile path toward the lake. Other than tonight's snow, the path was well packed from snow machines and ice fishermen dragging their gear sleds. The trail cut through a cathedral of red pine: tall, straight, big-barked trees with no lower limbs. Voices drifted up from the beach. An engine hummed. Firelight flickered beyond the trees and when I came around the bend, I caught sight of a flaming tepee of logs and brush.

A handful of people surrounded the bonfire, mugs or plates

in hand. To the fire's left, they'd set up a large tent with side-walls, the type you find at graduation parties. The engine noise came from a generator, extension cords running off its body and under the tent wall.

Closer to the tent I saw Ari, a huge fur hat covering his head. He tended a propane grill; steam rose off its lid where snow hit. Next to that was a snow-packed keg.

"Hello, hello," Ari called to me, his voice ebullient as ever. He waved me over. "Come, enjoy, partake of our feast."

I veered his way. His companion, Miriam Pohl, must have heard the greeting because she stepped through the tent flap.

"Vince," she called. "It's good to see you."

I waved and started to say something, but Ari interrupted.

"Vince Marshall?" Ari said. "So sorry that I didn't recognize you at first. You are doubly welcome, young man. Doubly. Look what you've done, man—this party you've created with your famous writing."

"Huh?"

"What Ari means is that since you wrote that feature story, his party has become rather popular," she said. "There are a lot more people here this year. I mean—"

"Look at this," he practically shouted. "It's a blizzard, it's midnight, and we've—"

"Yes, dear," Miriam said. "He knows all that."

She pulled back the tent's canvas flap and waved me inside. "Can I get you some coffee?"

"Coffee?" Ari said. "Get the man an espresso, or a cappuccino. Get the man some of those bacon-wrapped shrimps. Get him—"

We left Ari, still talking behind us. Inside I saw why they needed a generator. Two long tables were set up on the far wall. One held a buffet with flaming Sterno below silver pans. The other supported various small appliances, including an espresso machine. Two electric heaters warmed the room.

People talking and snacking sat at additional tables, their winter coats draped over the back of folding chairs. A couple nodded in my direction as I entered, enjoying the look of surprise on my face.

I didn't see Gina.

"Wow, Miriam," I said, thinking I should go back to my car and get the camera. "This is a little more upscale than last year."

"I told Ari I wasn't coming out here if it remained a bunch of freezing guys roasting pike over the fire on a forked stick. He resisted, but not too much."

Miriam, a master gardener and retired landscape architect, gave me her knowing smile. She'd volunteered for the last several years at the city's cemetery that Ari oversees. She's recently taken over directing the grounds crew and, with her own retirement stash, has turned the place into a veritable arboretum.

"Help yourself," she said. She lifted the lid off a serving pan. "We have coquille St. Jacques, sliced roast beef, and venison stew."

I felt like Pavlov's dog, my mouth literally watering at the smells.

"I'd love to," I said. "But I really came looking for Gina Holt. You know Gina, don't you? She works with me at the paper? Her truck is stuck in the snowbank up on the road."

"Sure, I know her. But I haven't seen her."

"She's wearing all purple. I figured she walked down here looking for someone to push her out."

"Let's check with Ari," she said.

We walked back out through the tent flap.

"Ari, have you seen a woman in a purple coat? She's stuck up on the road. Vince thought she may have come here for help."

"A damsel in distress, eh? A maiden in need of assistance?"

"Yes, Ari." She sighed and winked at me.

"Nope, haven't seen her." He closed the grill lid and strode toward the bonfire. "Hey good people," he yelled. "Has anyone in their revels seen a fair lady in purple? She's in need of assistance. She may have come down from the road seeking aid. Have you?"

I followed him and within a few steps enjoyed the fire's heat.

"Her car's stuck up in the road," I added, not sure if everyone could make sense of what Ari was saying.

He walked up to a couple who were planted in chairs, their legs reaching toward the flames.

"Hey, your hands are empty. We can't have that. This is a feast. Indulge in our spread. Partake or risk offending Miriam."

The couple begged off, claiming they'd just loosened their belts and couldn't stuff in another bite.

We circled the fire and then joined the revelers at the beach, asking again if anyone had seen Gina. No one had.

Two men were walking several hundred yards out on the frozen lake, checking their tip-ups, Ari told me. A lone partyer stood on the edge of the beach, outside of the fire's influence and wrapped in a ratty-looking fur coat. Ari chided her to come into the warmth and enjoy more food.

She waved a hand distractedly and kept scanning the lake.

"Not getting into the spirit," he stage-whispered as we turned back toward the bonfire and tent. After a few steps he added, "I don't believe she came here, Vince. Maybe she caught a ride from someone passing by."

"You're probably right."

"You want, I could get one of these boys with the big trucks to pull her out."

"Nah, her pickup's probably safer where it is until she's ready to move on. It's not blocking the road. I'll drive on to the next checkpoint. If she does show up, please let her know I was looking for her."

"Sure, sure, but I cannot allow you to leave without sustenance."

Ari slung an arm over my shoulder and pulled me inside the tent, where I let him brew me an espresso. The shot of caffeine would help get me through the night.

Chapter Ten

I left a note on Gina's dash and then headed west to the next checkpoint. The road conditions grew progressively worse, but I had a corridor of trees to guide me and to block the wind. The mushers would have a far greater challenge holding the line across the frozen chain of lakes and swamps.

At thirty minutes past midnight, I pulled into the Potlach Middle School parking lot. A front-end loader rumbled off to my left, dumping snow in a large mound. I followed its most recent plow line to a spot near Gord's sedan and parked. My cell crooned Lou's ringtone before I'd shut off the engine.

"How close are you to filing?" he snapped.

"I just pulled in to Potlach. Give me half an hour."

"I'll give you fifteen minutes," he said. "And keep it tight. We're packing a lot on the page."

"Have you heard from Gina?"

"Not since she bailed on us."

"She was at the last checkpoint and—"

"I thought she was sick."

"She left Dahinda ahead of me, Lou. I found her truck stuck in a snowbank about twenty miles east of here, but couldn't find her. I'm hoping she hitched a ride."

"I can't believe—"

"Give her a break, Lou."

"She should have just told me. Anyway, Mort says there are rumblings about calling the race."

"Because of the weather or the robbery?" I asked.

"The storm. It's not too bad here in Apostle Bay, but we're getting reports of roads drifting over and mushers having problems following the trail. The cops are talking about shutting down a few roads too."

"You think that might have more to do with corralling Earl Parsons?"

"Just ask around. We're hosed if they cancel ten minutes after I send the front page down."

When I hung up, my phone showed four messages. Two were from Lou, yelling at me, I'm sure, to not miss the deadline. Two were from Mom. I called, got her voice mail, and let her know all was good. I did the same for Deb. Then I grabbed my laptop and camera and headed for the building.

Most dog teams take the bulk of their mandatory rest in Potlach. Several handlers were spreading straw near their trucks or mixing five-gallon buckets of protein slop.

A female vet, bundled against the wind in a blue anorak, studied the pads and teeth of a dog team that had just arrived. Nearby, a race official poked through the triangular bag on Ally Tinknell's sled, making sure she carried the mandatory equipment. With twenty-five grand on the line, some mushers may be tempted to gain advantage by dropping the heavier items, such as an ax, stove, or wire cutters. The kit check keeps them honest.

"How's the trail, Ally?" the official asked.

"I've seen worse."

"Any trouble seeing trail markers?" he asked.

"No, but I've done 'er before and so's most of my team. They know the way. You're not thinking about calling it?"

"Not everyone's got a team that knows this trail, Ally."

"That's their problem," she said. "They shouldn't be out here if they can't cut it."

The official stood and handed over the clipboard for Tinknell's signature. "Everything looks good," he said. "There's coffee and food in the school cafeteria."

"Thanks," Ally said. "But my babies get fed first."

Inside the small cafeteria a third of the tables were filled with volunteers. I scanned for Gina on my way to the coffeepot, poured myself a cup, and then asked the grandmotherly volunteer where I could find the media center. She sent me to the school's library.

I made my way into the hall, passed lockers decorated with name acrostics, and found the room. Gord and a sheriff's deputy—still in a snowmobile suit like he'd just come in off the trail—conferred near the ham radio station. I waved. Gord nodded. Behind them I noticed Parsons' handler, Bishop. He sat at a round table nursing a Styrofoam cup.

The library was obviously once a classroom, now crammed full of waist-high bookshelves and a few small, round tables.

"What's the word on Parsons?" I asked Gord.

"Nothing yet."

"How's the trail?" I asked the deputy.

He shrugged noncommittally.

"Any truth to the rumor the race is going to be called off?"

"That's Ben Bowerman's decision," Gord said. He turned toward the man with headphones sitting in a fort of radio equipment. Behind the man, current race standings were shown on a chalkboard. I found Parsons' name. He had times listed through Dahinda, a couple of blank spaces, and then a time for Lake Margaret a little ahead of when I'd been there.

"So Parsons is still on the course?"

"Possibly," Gord said. "The radio operators are having trouble seeing the bib numbers in this storm."

"He'll be here," Bishop said. "He'll prove you're wrong."

"If he gets here, it won't prove anything but that he was getting cold," the deputy said.

"Why'd you drive the first leg?" I asked.

"Because he had food poisoning," Bishop said. "I already told the Keystone cops here, but they don't believe me."

"That's enough," Gord said.

"He told me to run the dogs and let him handle them."

"Then why'd you switch?" I asked.

Bishop shrugged his shoulders.

"And there it is," said the deputy, "the place where your story falls apart. Face it bud, he left you holding the bag. I'm gonna grab a Sloppy Joe, then I'm heading back out."

"Thanks for the update," Gord said.

I watched the deputy leave, and then asked Gord, "Have you seen Gina?"

He rolled his eyes. "Don't tell me she's covering this now too. Isn't she a little too close to it?"

"She's not working. I found her truck in a snowbank back at Lake Margaret, but she wasn't down at Ari's party. I thought she might have caught a ride here."

"I haven't seen her."

"I'm worried she might do something stupid."

"Like what?"

I shrugged. "Who knows? She's just not thinking clearly. Anyway, I'd better crank out a story before Lou has a stroke."

Across the room I set up base at a circular table that offered a clear view of the door and the radio operator. While my computer booted, I dropped to my knees and searched for a power outlet, wanting to conserve the battery for later. The gray carpet, worn by years of juvenile feet, didn't provide much in the way of cushion as I crawled along the wall.

I was backing out when the ham operator called, "Detective, we, uh . . . we have a situation. Some of the other mushers have found a team of dogs—"

Lou's ringtone sounded from my pocket.

"—but the rider is missing."

Chapter Eleven

Do you know what the heck is going on?" Lou asked.

"I just heard. I'll call you back in five, Lou."

"Wait—"

"I promise, in five," I said and closed the phone.

The phone chirped again and I saw it was Mom. I silenced it and crossed the room to hear what the radio operator was saying.

"—found some dogs tangled up in the tag alders," he said. Ben Bowerman, the deputy riding his heels, barreled through the library's door.

"Which team's missing?" Ben asked.

"We don't know yet," the operator said. "All we have are some dogs, still attached to their ganglines. It looks like they broke away. No one's found the sled or musher yet."

"For all we know, the musher could be miles back," Ben said. "Sometimes those dogs will keep running until something or someone snags 'em."

"Before you say any more," the deputy interrupted, "I think we ought to clear the room." He nodded in my direction.

Ben frowned at him.

"We have a rider missing. I'll take everyone's help."

"But—"

Ben turned back to the operator. "Who found the dogs and where are they now?"

"Teej Donovan found the team tangled up in the brush about

two miles west of Lake Margaret," the radio guy said. "Then Ron Sandusky—"

I looked at the board and saw that Sandusky was bib fourteen.

"—came along. They did a quick search but said the snow's blowing so much they couldn't even follow tracks. Teej stayed with the team. Ron went back to Lake Margaret to get help. I guess they rounded up a couple of snowmobiles and those are out on the trail now, looking for the sled and musher."

Lou's ringtone sounded. I silenced it as quickly as possible.

Ben turned to the deputy. "Get Search and Rescue back there to help."

"Don't you think—"

"No, I don't," Ben interrupted. "Get your men out there."

"Ben, you have to admit there's a possibility this is Parsons' team and that he ditched them on purpose," Gord said.

"There is no way!" Bishop shouted. "If—"

"Until I learn different," Ben said, "I have to go on the assumption that I have a rider missing and possibly hurt. We'll do everything we can to find him or her."

Ben turned back to the deputy. "Why are you waiting? Go!"

The deputy glanced to Gord, who nodded his agreement, pulled his cell from a hip holster, and then walked away from us to speak privately.

My cell phone rang again. I saw Mom's number on the screen.

"Turn that thing off," Ben growled. "Or take it out of here."

I silenced the call and switched my phone to vibrate.

Ben, meanwhile, spun back to the radio operator. "Is there any way you can get a radio at the scene?"

"We're working on it."

"Thanks. Keep me posted. I'm going to the cafeteria to see what kind of help I can round up."

"What about the race?" the radio guy asked. "Is it still on?"

"For now let's just see if we can find who those dogs belong to and get everyone else to Potlach safely."

My phone buzzed. I expected to see the *Chronicle*'s number on the screen—Lou would be apoplectic by now—but it was Deb's. I moved away from the chaos and flipped it open.

"Vince?" It was Mom. "Where are you? I've been trying to reach you all night."

"I'm in Potlach. What's wrong?"

"It's Deb. We're at the hospital."

I walked to the far corner of the library, away from the noise.

"What do you mean you're at the hospital?"

"Don't panic," Mom said. "She didn't even want me to call you."

"What's wrong?"

"Deb fainted. But she's okay now."

"Where? When?"

"At your home, Vince. After we left the café. Deb said she was getting a cramp in her side. It hurt enough that she had trouble getting out of the car. Then, I don't know if it was coming in out of the cold or what, but she just collapsed through your front door. She hit that little table in your hall and cut her forehead."

"But—"

"I tried calling you. And I left a message at the newspaper too."

I cringed.

"Sorry, Mom, there's no signal between here and Dahinda."

"We figured that," she said.

The earliest I could get home would be three, maybe four in the morning.

"Deb didn't even want me to bring her to the emergency room," Mom continued. "But I insisted. It wasn't that bad, but she definitely needed a few stitches."

"If she only needed a few stitches, why are you still at the hospital?"

"It's . . . it's just a precaution," she said.

"A precaution for what?"

I had an unreasonable desire to go find Ben and yell at him for being away from the emergency room. Since he was here with the race, Deb was probably in the care of some intern right now.

"It can wait until you're here," Mom said.

"What's that supposed to mean?"

"It means that Deb wants to talk with you privately, but that it's nothing critical and can wait until the roads clear. So be smart, or I'll regret that I called you."

I dropped into a wooden library chair and closed my eyes—a mistake because I envisioned Deb in a hospital bed with her head swathed in bandages.

"I'm on my way."

"No," Mom said. "The highway along Lake Superior is closed."

"Closed? It's not that bad of a storm."

"It's drifting, that's why. Listen, there's absolutely nothing you can do. Deb's sleeping. Glory's sleeping. I'm here with them. I just wanted to let you know they were okay in case you got the earlier messages. I'll call you the minute Deb wakes up. I promise."

I leaned back, trying to decide. If I started back now, I'd be out of touch for the next couple of hours.

"Okay, please call the minute she wakes," I said. I looked toward the radio table. Gord was still there. He'd know about any road closings.

"Don't worry," Mom said.

Storm or not, I planned to leave now if Gord told me the road was open.

I closed my phone and it rang again—Lou calling. I silenced the phone and tried to wrap my mind around Mom's words, but didn't have a chance, as a race volunteer burst through the door.

"Detective," he shouted. "Doc Bowerman says they need you outside. Right away."

Gord followed the man out. I packed my computer and gear and took up the chase.

Chapter Twelve

I joined the cluster of people pushing through the cafeteria's exit doors.

"What's going on?"

"Some kind of standoff," a guy said.

The stream of people carried me outside. We were on the lee side of the building, protected from a wind that whistled across the roof. We moved as a group toward the race checkpoint, where a crowd loosely surrounded a dog team. The musher held her lead dog, a black husky, by its harness. The dog stood on its hind legs, straining against the lead toward Ben Bowerman. He held his hands, palms up, in a placating gesture.

Lupine Ryder, wearing a blue parka with the hood pushed back and snow-crusted goggles on her forehead, shouted for the crowd to stay back. Her handler, the young woman Gina had been trying to corral in Dahinda, held on to the sled.

Behind the sled and at the edge of the crowd, I saw Sunny D'light crouched on the ground and trying to unload her video camera from its bulky bag. Sunny is Lucy Demott's replacement at the local TV station and Sunny D' is not her real name. It's Gertrude Millimaki. Sunny told me at our first meeting that she aspired to a job as a Weather Channel storm chaser and somehow she's managed to work a weather-related angle into each of her news stories.

"This is ridiculous!" Lupine yelled. "I've been set up!"

I moved closer and pulled the lens cap off my camera.

"Nobody has accused you, Ms. Ryder," Ben said.

"Yeah, right."

Ben inched closer. Gord emerged on Lupine's other side and Ben signaled for him to stay back.

"C'mon, Ms. Ryder," Ben said. "Your dogs have had a hard night. They deserve a rest and some food. This isn't helping them."

"The dogs are fine!" she shouted. "They could run you over and take me out of here right now."

"I'm sure they could, but why would you want to do that?"

"Because somebody set me up!"

"Let's take care of your dogs and then we'll figure it out."

Lupine scanned the crowd again.

"You think I'm an idiot?"

"Ms. Ryder—"

"I don't know how those things got in my kit."

Ben stepped forward again and Lupine's dog lunged against its lead.

"I'm tired of shouting over this wind and getting snow down my neck," Ben said. "And to be honest, right now I really don't care what we found in your bag. We have a lost, possibly injured musher out on that trail and I'm much more concerned about him or her. So if you want to run out of here, be my guest."

"Who's lost?"

"We don't know yet. A team of dogs were caught in some tag alders west of Lake Margaret. We haven't found the sled or musher yet. So, unless you have some information that will help me. . . ."

I snapped a few quick photos and then stuck the camera under my coat.

"Unbelievable," she said. "It's got to be him."

"Who?" Ben asked.

"Earl," she said.

"How do you know?"

My phone vibrated. I pulled it out, figuring it was Mom, but it was Lou, so I stuffed it back in my pocket.

"This is all his doing," she said.

Other than the lead dog, which had remained focused on Ben, the rest of her team seemed to be relaxing. A wheel dog, one of two closest to the sled, wasn't even looking at the crowd, but was instead licking the sled bag. Dogs often ate snow for hydration and I figured this dog was doing something similar.

Someone in the crowd yelled that another headlamp was approaching, but no one moved toward the chute.

"Folks, clear out. This show's over," Ben said. Directing his gaze at Lupine's handler, he asked, "Where's your truck?"

She glanced at Lupine, waiting for permission, and then pointed.

"C'mon, people," Ben shouted. "Make room. Give these dogs a little breathing space."

Ben turned back to Lupine. "We'll meet you at your truck and give you a hand."

He signaled for Gord to follow and then kept walking in the direction Lupine's handler had pointed. Lupine watched them, but she didn't move.

Ben turned once and motioned them forward.

"C'mon," he shouted. "There are other teams coming in."

"We don't need your help at the truck!" Lupine shouted.

"Maybe not with the dogs," Ben said. "But my friend Gordon here is big enough to scare away any distractions while you feed them. We'll talk after that."

"What's to keep me from just taking off?" Ryder said.

Ben shrugged his shoulders and continued toward the musher camps.

"We'd find you," Gord said over his shoulder.

"Fat chance," Lupine muttered.

Ben put a hand on Gord's back and said something, but I couldn't hear it through the wind. Ben then turned and walked back toward the school as if he'd already forgotten about Lupine. Gord kicked his way forward through deepening snow toward the Nightshade Kennels truck.

"What are you waiting for?" Lupine shouted at her handler. "Pull the hook free and let's go." With her hand still on the lead dog's harness, she led her team in Gord's path.

Ben stopped briefly in front of a race official in an orange bib. The man handed him a bag.

"Well, that was kind of crazy," the man next to me said. He too wore the orange volunteer bib. He slapped his hands together to get some blood flowing.

"What was it all about?"

"During the mandatory bag check we found a couple of interesting things in her kit."

I waited for him to elaborate, but it became obvious he wanted me to ask.

"Such as?"

"The Superior Cup, for one," he said, enjoying the surprised look I gave him. "And a bloody ax."

Chapter Thirteen

I climbed into my Bronco and, still unsure what to do, called Lou.

"Sorry to push you off earlier," I said. "Things got really crazy."

"I gathered that. Where are you with copy?"

"Not even started," I said. I gave him a rundown of the discovery of the stolen cup and bloody ax.

Lou didn't respond at first and I checked to see if the signal was lost.

"Looks like our deadline's blown," he said. "Okay, put something together quick, and tie it in with the race cancellation and search for—"

"Cancellation?" I interrupted.

"You didn't know?"

"It was still on when I left the building."

Lou yelled something to Mort Maki, got a response, and then said: "It's definitely canceled. Bowerman made the call moments ago, partly because of the weather, but mostly to aid the search for Earl Parsons."

"Parsons? They found the sled?"

"Yep, about a mile back from the dogs. It's Parsons' sled, but no sign of him. I guess the plan is to stop all mushers when they reach Potlach."

"That's interesting. Lupine Ryder said Parsons was missing. And if I heard her right, she was blaming him for the stolen cup being found in her bag."

"How's that?" Lou asked.

"I have no clue."

"Ask around and see what you can scare up in the next fifteen to twenty minutes. Call me back then and I'll decide what we can roll with."

"Uh, yeah. Only one problem. I really hate to dump this on you, Lou, but I just got a call and Deb's in the hospital. I'm heading back to Apostle Bay."

"You can't," Lou said.

"Excuse me? This is my wife."

"That's not what I meant," he said. "The state police have closed the road between Dahinda and Apostle Bay. You can't get through."

"This is an emergency. They'll let me."

"You know different," he said. "No one gets around those roadblocks. What happened to Deb?"

"I don't know for sure. She passed out, hit her head. My mom's with her now. Anyway, I can drive to Dahinda and wait there for the road to open."

"Hold on," Lou said.

He started talking with someone, but I couldn't make out what they were saying. I flipped the ignition key halfway and let the wipers try to clear the windshield, but it was fogged up and I couldn't see anyway.

"Vince?"

"Yeah."

"Obviously it's your call, but you won't do Deb any good if you end up in the ditch or worse—"

"Lou, I'm going,"

"—and Mort is getting one of the ham operators over to the hospital. He'll find your mother, and they can keep you posted."

"But—"

"Mort says his man can be transmitting from there in fifteen, twenty minutes tops. You hit the road now and you'll be out of touch."

"It wouldn't be right for me to stay here."

He let me think about it. I started the engine to get some heat going, but knew he was right.

"Cripes! Okay, I'll wait by the radio."

"Good," he said. "Holmes dug up the obit on Amy Parsons and some of the old articles on the bank robbery. He'll fax all of it to you. If you're stuck there, might as well keep your mind active."

"Yeah, right."

"Oh, and get me a comment from Bowerman while you're at it," he said. "I'll look for your call in fifteen minutes."

"Thanks," I said again, torn between feeling grateful and used.

Chapter Fourteen

I cut the engine and called Mom.

"How's Deb?" I asked.

"She and Glory are still sleeping. How are things in Potlach?"

I gave her a brief rundown and told her about the radio operator headed her way.

"I'm not kidding. It's how Lou got me to stay a while longer. But as soon as they reopen the road, I'm coming back."

"We're not going anywhere," she said. "And I'll watch for your ham radio guy."

Next I grabbed my camera and headed toward the musher staging area. I'd snap more photos of Lupine, try for a few comments, and then head inside to collect my fax from Lou and camp out by the radio.

On my way, I ran into Sunny D' setting up her tripod.

"Hey, Sunny," I called. "I've got to get back to Apostle Bay ASAP. Can you tell me when this storm is going to let up?"

"Right now there's a low pressure system moving across the Dakotas and that's going to—"

"Forget the gory details about weather fronts," I interrupted. "I just want an ETA of when it will clear enough for them to reopen the road between Dahinda and Apostle Bay."

She sighed. "Probably by sunrise. The wind has already shifted."

"Thanks." I started away and then turned back. "You know Ben called the race, right?"

"Yeah," she answered. She swung her camera up onto the tripod and locked it in. "I'm trying to get a shot of the snow, the way it's blowing off the roof of the building over there. It'll make good B-roll."

"If I was you, I'd shoot some B-roll of the Nightshade Kennels truck."

"Really? What a great idea," she said.

The look in her eyes told me that she'd already done it, and that she thought I was a patronizing dolt for suggesting something so obvious.

I yanked my zipper up tight to my chin and headed toward Lupine's truck. A twelve-dog team coming from the chute area trotted past, the dogs' tongues hanging long. A few bent and scooped snow with their mouths.

At most camps the dogs were tethered to a bar attached to a trailer hitch. They lay in hay or stood gulping food at metal bowls. Handlers and mushers were checking the dogs' feet or the sled gear. At one truck a musher lay wrapped in a sleeping bag under his or her truck's bed, sleeping in the hay with the team. A few dogs lifted an eyelid as I walked past, or twitched an ear, but for the most part they ignored me. No one spoke in more than a grunt or nod of the head. Mushers are quiet by nature, and at this stage they're also dead tired.

Lupine's truck was parked next to Teej and Erin Donovan's rig. Erin was helping Bella Ryder feed dogs. Two race volunteers stood off to one side, stamping their feet and hands and looking embarrassed.

"Hey, Erin," I called. Lupine's lead dog, the black one, stood, stretched its chain taut, and growled. I saw the hackles up on its neck. I halted and put my hands up in surrender. Bella stepped forward and whispered to the dog. She called it Larkspur, and it settled back into its bed of hay but kept an eye on me.

"Vince is harmless," Erin said. "Any news?"

"I haven't been inside yet," I said. "But the word is that Ben canceled the race—"

"We heard," she said.

"—and the loose dog team belonged to Earl Parsons."

"Yeah, heard that too. Earl's been mushing his whole life. He should be able to survive a winter storm."

"Is Teej still out there, helping with the search?" I asked.

"Yep. So are a lot of the other mushers."

"Then between the search and rescue folks and all the volunteer help, they ought to find Earl soon."

"Let's hope," Erin said.

"Where's Lupine? Inside with the cops?"

Erin nodded. Bella looked up from the dogs and glared at me.

"Lupine didn't steal that cup," she said. "I'd know."

Erin pointed over her shoulder with a thumb. "These guys are supposed to be watching Bella, to make sure she doesn't take off or something. That's why I came over. I know they don't mean it, but they're not too welcoming."

"Is Bella short for Belladonna?" I asked.

"I was named after my mom's first lead dog."

"Yes, the poisonous flower theme. Whose idea was that?"

"What's it to you?"

"Just curious," I said. "It's different."

"They've got an all-female team," Erin said. "Bella here's just fourteen years old and probably the best handler out here. She's got a special way with the dogs."

"Fourteen? How do you drive?"

"Same way you do," she said.

"Probably better," Erin added.

"I meant—"

"I know what you meant," the girl said. She left it at that.

"Is an all-female team rare?" I asked.

Erin nodded a confirmation.

"It shouldn't be," Bella said. "Lupine says it's better because there are no distractions. The females of all species are more focused."

"Isn't that the truth," Erin said.

I glanced at the two race officials and decided that maybe they were more intimidated than Erin and Bella.

"Well, they're beautiful dogs," I said.

"Fast too," Bella said. "It's a real shame they're not going to let us finish the race. The girls were running great."

"Well, besides the weather and the missing musher, there is the little problem with the stuff they found in your mom's kit. I'm not so sure you'd still be racing anyway."

"Someone set her up," she said.

"Well, doesn't matter now anyway," Erin said. "Ben Bowerman was right; the first priority is everyone's safety, and that includes the race volunteers as well as the teams."

"My mom says people need to take care of themselves, not count on others."

"I've been wondering, Bella: why would someone want to frame your mother?"

"Vince," Erin interrupted. "She's just—"

"What, I'm just a kid? It's sabotage, plain and simple. Someone doesn't want us to win."

"Really? Is it that cutthroat? I mean, between the mushers?"

Erin shook her head no. Bella said, "Some people don't like that my mom wins so often."

"Have you done the Iditarod?"

"We didn't want to race it until we knew we had a team that could win it. And we do now. These girls are the best runners we've ever had, and this was supposed to be our qualifying race. That's another reason someone might have sabotaged us, to keep us out."

As unlikely as that was, I thought I'd better not disagree. The look Erin gave me confirmed that.

Bella went back to feeding her dogs. I stepped farther away and Erin followed.

"How could someone set them up?" I whispered. "Lupine didn't even stop in Dahinda. She just slowed down enough to sign the log."

Erin shrugged. "What's more important is what's going to happen to Bella," she said. "If Lupine is arrested, she can't stay on her own. She's just a kid."

Bella continued ministering to the dogs and checking over her shoulder, looking toward the school, presumably for Lupine to return. Erin turned back toward Bella.

"Hey, Bella, since my team isn't here yet, I'd be glad to stay with your team for a little bit while you go inside, grab a bite to eat, and look for your mom."

"My mom told me to stick here no matter what. She doesn't want anyone poking around our stuff. Plus, these girls are the most valuable things we own. I've got to protect them."

I watched her stroke another of the dogs.

"How do you handle doing all this and schoolwork too?" I asked. "It must be quite a load."

"I'm homeschooled," Bella said. "These girls are my teachers. You can learn more from dogs than from some government-paid teacher trying to brainwash you."

Erin raised an eyebrow and we exchanged a glance.

"Do you have anything to eat in that truck?" Erin asked. "It's been a long night and you've got to keep your strength up too."

"I ain't hungry," Bella said.

"But—"

"I've got stuff if I get hungry," she said. She took a harness from the truck, removed a glove, and with her bare hand, started inspecting it for flaws.

"My friend said you look like someone she knows," I said. "She tried to talk with you back in Dahinda, but you had to run."

"That crazy lady?" she asked.

"Yeah, her name is Gina."

"Whatever," Bella said. "She said I looked like her daughter or something. She's nuts. I was born and raised in Canada. Don't know what was up with that."

Bella's lead dog growled and stood. We followed its gaze to Gord, headed our way with a Styrofoam cup in each gloved hand.

The two volunteers went up to him, no doubt thinking he'd brought them coffee. He chatted with them for a moment and then nodded his head back toward the building. They thanked him and followed his tracks back in that direction.

"Any word on the search for Parsons?" I asked.

"Nada," he said.

He handed Erin a cup. "Chicken noodle soup," he said. "I brought one for you too, Bella."

Bella ignored him.

"I'll hold hers," Erin said.

I took his arm and steered him away from their camp.

"How about Lupine?" I asked. "What's she saying?"

"Not a thing you could print," he said, heading back in Erin's direction.

"Thanks for staying with her, Erin," Gord said. "I'm trying to get some help here, but . . ." He gestured toward the sky.

"It's not a problem," Erin said. "What's happening with the search for Earl?"

"Not much yet. But there are plenty of people helping, so I think we'll find him soon."

"Have you heard anything about Teej?" Erin asked.

"He's out there with them, I know that. But I haven't spoken directly with him."

"If you do hear something . . ."

"I'll make sure to get word to you, okay?" Gord said.

Gord started back to the school and I followed. The sky to our left was growing lighter and I realized the wind was down from before.

"What are you going to do with Lupine?" I asked.

"We've got to work it out with the sheriff."

"Turf problems?"

"No, logistics. I'm leaving it to the chief to work out. Lupine is not the most cooperative suspect we've ever had."

"Understandable, given her perspective. Who's with her now, the deputy?"

"Potlach Village's chief. He's got two part-time officers, but their other job is plowing, so they're tied up at the moment."

"What about her daughter? What's the plan for her?"

"The handler? I'd wondered if that was her daughter. Lupine wouldn't even tell us that."

"Well, she is the daughter, and guess what? She's only four-teen."

Gord stopped. We were a dozen yards from the cafeteria door and a couple of volunteers came through carrying steaming cups.

"Fourteen? Great." Gord shook his head and started forward again. "Guess I'll need to get someone from Child and Family out here too. Can this turn into any more of a mess?"

"What about the bloody ax?" I asked.

Gord reached for the door handle, but it swung open before he grabbed it and almost popped him in the face. Sunny D' came through.

"Bloody ax?" she said. "What about the bloody ax?"

"I said, when's that bloody fax coming in? I'm waiting for something from my office."

"Don't be a jerk," she said.

"Why?" Gord quipped. "He's so good at it."

My phone rang and it was Deb's ringtone.

"It's Deb," I said. "I'll catch up to you."

I flipped open the phone as I went through the door, and then veered right to a private corner.

"Hi." I was out of breath.

"Hey, were you running?"

"Just trying to get inside. You okay?"

"I'm fine," she said.

"That's not what Mom tells me. What's going on?"

"I was coming in from the cold and the heat got to me, made me a little light-headed. I told her not to call you."

"Uh-huh, just light-headed? What did the doctor say?"

"We can talk when you get home."

"The road's closed, but the storm's letting up. I'll try to be there for breakfast. How's Glory?"

"She's sleeping. And you're lying about the weather. I hear it's terrible."

"No, the wind's dying off. Sunny D' says there's a high pressure area moving this way."

"How's the race going?" she asked.

"It's not," I said. "Ben called it off. One musher is missing and there's a rescue operation under way. Officials found the stolen gold cup in another musher's sled along with an unexplainable bloody ax. And being out in the boonies, there's a shortage of police to deal with it all, and nobody's sure who is in charge. So it's, you know, business as usual."

"Oh," she said. The amount of disappointment that she put in that one word crushed me.

"I'm on my way, Deb."

"No, that's—"

"I'm on my way. The cops can escort me if they won't open the road."

"But—"

"I'll call you when I reach Dahinda," I said.

"Please be careful, Vince."

"No worries."

"Vince? I really need you. Thanks."

I turned a 180 and jogged to my Bronco.

Chapter Fifteen

I pushed the speed as much as I dared on the snow-packed road. As Sunny D' predicted, the wind faded, and I was hoping the snowplows would have the highway open by the time I reached Dahinda.

An occasional musher truck passed me, heading in the opposite direction—toward Potlach. A state police SUV blew by in a cloud of white powder, probably reinforcements for Gord and the village chief. Not far behind the cops, a familiar sky blue pickup almost ran me off the road. I slowed and watched Gina in my rearview mirror. I flipped open my phone to call her, but no signal.

It was a solitary drive after that until I reached Lake Margaret, where a line of parked trucks narrowed the road. I could barely squeeze through without dragging my mirror along someone's cab. At a gap between two trucks, Ari and another man, equally as big, were gesturing at each other.

I stopped and rolled down my passenger window. Teej turned and greeted me.

"Any word on Parsons yet?" I asked.

"Nothing," Teej said.

"Teej here is the one who found the dogs," Ari said.

"Barking like crazy they were, right beside the trail, snagged in some tag alders," Teej said. "Drew my dogs off the trail and the next thing I know, we were all tangled together in a big mess."

"What do you think happened?"

"Who knows?" Teej said. "Earl could have fallen off the sled or a gangline could have broken, since the dogs chew on them all the time."

"Two years ago we had dogs and a sled come strolling into the party with no rider," Ari said. "The musher came running along about an hour later. His dogs probably would have trotted right on to Potlach if they hadn't smelled the food."

"Really?"

"Sure," Teej said. "Especially if they're following a trail or scenting the other dogs. Although I'd have guessed Earl's team was too disciplined. I'm almost thinking maybe one of his dogs got injured or something and he'd stopped to treat it. Or maybe he was trying to load the dog in his bag or something. The kit was all torn up, like maybe the dog had struggled. There was some blood too. Could be the injured dog went berserk and all the others wound up in a fight. We won't know until Earl turns up."

"You seem confident he will."

"Any musher worth his salt can take care of himself. Earl's hunkered down somewhere waiting for daylight."

A truck pulled up behind me and honked.

"Erin's worried sick about you, Teej," I said, ignoring the truck. "You better get in touch with her somehow and let her know you're okay."

"That woman, always worrying."

"I'm serious."

"Yeah, I know. I'll get them radio guys to give her a call."

The truck behind me honked again. I waved and started toward Dahinda.

Everyone seemed confident of Earl's survival skills, but I wondered, if he was so good, why'd he lose his team in the first place?

Chapter Sixteen

By the time I cleared the National Forest, state cops had reopened the highway. I stopped briefly at an all-night party store, blew two bucks on an energy drink, and called Deb.

She had convinced my mom to bring her and Glory home, only to face more bad news: egg yolks and spray paint dripping down our cedar siding and snowmobile tracks circling our yard. Adding to her stress was the ham operator who'd followed them home. Deb said she wasn't sure if it was out of a sense of duty or if he wanted food, but the guy wasn't taking the hint to leave.

I called Lou next, expecting him to blow up, but he was eerily calm and told me they got the front page done without me. The search for Parsons was expanding as more rescue personnel and volunteers arrived near Lake Margaret. Ari's beach party was now search headquarters and the radio operators were on-site, coordinating efforts. Mort was tapped into everything. The police were mum on Lupine.

Lou told me to handle what I needed to at home and check in by midday if possible. I said a silent prayer of thanks for his newfound temper control.

An hour later I pulled into my driveway, parking next to an Apostle Bay patrol car. As usual, there was less snow accumulation in Apostle Bay, where the harbor seems to offer protective cover.

My headlamps shone on bright red graffiti gracing our garage door—a nasty invective directed at Deb. Snowmobile tracks ran around our house like a war party had been circling. Egg yolks dotted our cabin windows.

We'd been through some up-and-down times in Apostle Bay. It's a small town. Everyone knows everyone else's business. You read the *Chronicle*'s court page and you might see your neighbor or co-worker. People disagreed with you and said so in public meetings. But this . . . this was the first time someone had violated our home.

Mom came through the door and across the yard toward me. "What the—"

"Deb's inside with Archie Freeman," she said. "C'mon."

"Can you believe this?"

"No, I can't."

"Man, when I find—"

"Come inside," she said.

She grabbed my arm and led me up the front steps and into the house. I found Deb, her colleague Tony Wittmer, and Detective Archie Freeman in our living room.

"Papa!" Glory screamed, launching herself at me from the hallway.

I scooped Glory into my arms, gave her a quick squeeze, and saw Deb over her shoulder. My wife was pale, exhausted. I carried Glory into the room and grabbed Deb, trying to apologize with the strength of my hug.

Freeman coughed.

"Like I was saying . . ."

I gave Deb another squeeze, and then keeping a hand on her shoulder, turned to Freeman. "What the heck happened?"

"I think that's obvious," Freeman said.

Freeman and I have had an uneasy truce of late. Basically

that means we haven't crossed each other's paths. He thinks I act like rules don't apply to me. I believe the same of him.

"Your wife stirred the pot and this—"

"Whoa," I interrupted. "Back up. My wife spent the night in the hospital and someone trashed our house. That's a crime no matter what your personal beef is with me. What are you doing about it?"

"Calm down, Marshall. I'm not blaming her. I'm just saying it appears to be the work of someone who has issues with your wife's involvement in the snowmobile ordinance. That's all."

"Someone who has issues? Give me a break. This isn't like TP-ing someone's house, or knocking over their mailbox. This is way over the line."

"Vince, he's—" Mom started.

"Mom, it's a civics class. If someone is crazy enough to spray-paint our house over a lesson plan, then there is a very disturbed individual or group running loose out there. Freeman should be out finding them, not sitting in my house telling us we asked for it."

"This is obviously blowback from the vandalism to the snowmobile trails," Freeman said. "And there are some who think your wife's encouraging that."

Wittmer moved his lanky frame off the couch and toward Freeman.

"I've been telling you that's nonsense for the last half hour," he said.

"Although what they did to your house"—Freeman pointed toward our front window, where the remnants of two eggs had frozen to the glass—"is unpleasant, no one got hurt. But out on the trail, if someone hits one of those surprise barricades, or is clotheslined by a wire strung across the trail—they're dead. So let's keep it in perspective here."

Mom said, "Archie, I think—"

"Forget it, Mom," I said. "It's not worth it. Go find someone else to harass, Freeman."

With Glory still on my hip, I steered Deb out of our living room, leaving Mom and Wittmer to see the detective out. I just wanted to forget about the vandalism and the race for the moment and find out what was really going on with Deb.

Chapter Seventeen

Our house, once my parents' cabin, had been remodeled for year-round living when we moved to Apostle Bay. As a cabin, there were few closets, and we relied on two dressers and a wardrobe to store our clothing. I'd once thought it romantic that we couldn't pass each other in the room without hugging, but these days it seemed more like we were getting in each other's way as we raced to the next thing.

Deb slumped onto the bed, grabbed a tangled quilt, and covered herself. Glory, still wearing yesterday's black Winnie the Pooh sweatshirt and tights, climbed in next to her and gave her a hug.

I heard voices from the living room, and then the front door opened and closed. Mom called for Glory to come help her make some muffins, and I appreciated that she knew I needed time alone with Deb. I shooed Glory out and closed the bedroom door.

As soon as she'd left, Deb buried her face in a pillow and started crying. That alone was enough out of character that I knew I hadn't heard the worst. I slipped onto the bed beside her, wrapped an arm around her as best I could, and let her have it out.

When Deb reined in the tears, she pushed herself up and grabbed a tissue off the dresser. Then she sat against the backboard and looked at me.

"So, I'm guessing you didn't just faint from a little light-headedness," I said.

"I had a miscarriage," she said.

"I, uh . . . are you, okay?"

Deb nodded. "I'll go back to my doctor Monday, for a fol-low-up. But yeah, I'm fine. Surprised, but fine."

"Yeah, surprised. Wow."

I knew I should be concerned about Deb's health and that I should ask other questions, but all I could think was that we hadn't been planning to have another child, at least not to my knowledge. Things were finally settling down. Glory was be-coming more independent and sleeping more regularly. Our jobs were going better than in the past. Life was starting to settle down. Deb obviously read all that in my face.

"I didn't know I was pregnant," Deb said.

"Me either," I said, wishing as soon as the words left my mouth I could retrieve them.

"That's why I haven't felt good, and why I passed out," she said.

"Does this mean, um, can we . . . you know?"

"Have more children? Yes. Apparently this is more com-mon than I realized. The emergency room doctor says it's a natural process—my body's way of taking care of me, I guess."

Deb choked up again. I handed her another tissue and tried to wrap my mind around this.

"I'm sorry, Deb. I'm so, so sorry."

She wiped the latest tears and turned toward me.

"You're not mad?"

"Mad? Why would I be mad? Oh, Deb, this is horrible."

"I was afraid you'd be upset, you know, because . . ."

We held each other for a few more moments and then I pushed her back and told her how much I loved her. It sounded lame, I know, but it was the best thing I knew to do.

Later, when we'd both stopped crying, Deb explained a little more to me. She'd be fully recovered in a few days and this shouldn't affect future pregnancies, if we decided to have another child.

"I guess this explains why Mom was acting goofy," I said.

"She's been great. I don't know how we'd have made it through last night without her."

"Deb, I'm so sorry I left for Dahinda last night. I should have taken you home from the diner."

"I told you to go. Besides, there's no way you could've known," Deb said.

Glory burst through the door.

"Food is ready!" she shouted. "We made you chicken soup for your soul!"

Deb smiled, wiped her eyes once more, and then took Glory's hand. As they left our room I couldn't help thinking that Glory would be a wonderful big sister—someday.

Chapter Eighteen

I was scheduled to work the desk Saturday night, and there was no way to beg off since Gina was still incommunicado. We sent Glory to stay with my mom in case the vandals returned. Deb invited a few girlfriends over to commiserate— and because it made me feel more comfortable that she wasn't home alone.

On my way to the office, I called Lou for an update. The state police had a cold-water dive team on the way to Lake Margaret, apparently now believing Earl may have gone through thin ice at a place where there was a spring. The storm had passed and most roads were now clear. Lou sent me to check the police dispatch log before coming to the *Chronicle*.

The night shift officer buzzed me through security when I arrived at police headquarters in the basement of City Hall.

"Is Gord available?" I asked.

"He's in a meeting with the chief," the officer said. "Why don't you wait in the conference room? There's a fresh pot of Joe brewing—fair trade, organic, pretty sweet stuff."

"How does that work into the city's budget?"

"An anonymous donation arrives in the mail each month," he said. "A subscription to some kind of coffee service. Seems like someone out there actually likes us."

I did like them, but the real reason I'd been upgrading their Java was selfish—Gord's coffee gave me heartburn.

"Probably some elderly person whose cat you rescued," I said.

"Here's to old ladies and their cats." He toasted with his mug. "You know the way, right?"

I strolled to the conference room, surprised to find it occupied by a man: white hair, reading glasses halfway down his nose, beige corduroy sports coat with elbow patches, and a crossword puzzle in his hand. He glanced over the lenses and I half expected him to pull out a pipe and tobacco pouch just to finish off the 1960s professor look.

"You're Doc Marshall's son," he said.

I sighed. "Yep. Let me guess: either he was your doctor, or he delivered your child."

"Everyone has a Doc Marshall story, don't they?"

"Seems like it," I said. "How did you know him?"

"He worked for me on occasion."

I slid into a chair. "Doing what?"

"Medical examiner."

I knew most of the cops but didn't recognize this guy. It must have shown on my face.

"Retired FBI," he said. "Steve Olsen."

He leaned across and offered his hand.

"So what brings a retired G-man here on a Saturday night?"

"I like to keep in touch with old friends."

"Uh-huh," I said. "The bank robbery was your case, wasn't it? Bank robberies always involve the feds."

He shrugged.

"How long have you been retired?"

"Five, six years."

He tapped his pencil on the table. Voices murmured out in the hall. Olsen then stood and went to the coffeepot for a refill.

"Good coffee," he said. "Thanks."

"What for?"

He returned to his seat.

"The coffee. Your godfather says you buy it."

"He's crazy," I said.

"Yeah, that sounds like Dale. Crazy like a fox."

He returned, sat on the edge of the table, and sipped his mug.

"You're here to see Dale?" he asked.

"Nah, Gordon Greenleaf. I want the latest on Earl Parsons and Lupine Ryder for tomorrow's edition."

"Are you expecting much?"

"Not really, but it's my job to try. Since we're both killing time, how about you refreshing my memory on the robbery?"

He smiled. "As long as it's just two guys shooting the breeze, I'll tell you what I can remember.

"The Earl Parsons of this world always screw up," Olsen started. It seemed rehearsed and I got the feeling he'd been waiting all night to say it. "You just have to wait them out because somewhere down the road, they always blow it."

"So, there's no question he robbed the bank?"

"None. There was, as we say, a preponderance of evidence."

"And his irrefutable alibi?"

Olsen waved it away. "A doddering fool who couldn't keep track of what day it was."

"Then why—"

He shrugged. "Why wasn't he prosecuted? No backbone, that's why."

"You know what I don't get?" I said. "Why go through the trouble of wearing a mask, and then drive your easily recognizable truck? It seems plain stupid."

Olsen chuckled. "Stupidity born of desperation. He was in big-time debt, no money in the bank, maxed-out credit."

"Nothing to lose?"

"That's right," he said. "He got a teller at gunpoint, had

her clean out her drawer and then the other drawers. It wasn't—"

"How much did he get?"

Olsen's eyes narrowed and I got the message: quit interrupting.

"He left the bank with about four grand. These fools never realize how little money tellers have in their drawers. He panicked, ran out the door, jumped in his truck, sideswiped another car, and drove away."

"What about his wife, Amy? I heard she was in the truck too."

"She was. Witnesses saw her while he was inside the bank. One witness said she was a prisoner, that her hands were taped together and she had on a gag. But I'd bet my pension she was in on it. She was probably supposed to drive the getaway vehicle."

"But she didn't?"

"She froze. Later he got rid of her. It makes sense. The consensus among people we interviewed was that she was a major pain in the you-know-where. The evidence showed she was probably the one who spent them into oblivion in the first place. I can tell you this for sure: Parsons didn't show a single ounce of remorse over her disappearance."

"You said he spent the money?"

"Right after the U.S. attorney dropped the charges, Parsons hit the road. He moved to Northern Minnesota and hunkered down. He bought forty acres and paid cash. His place is twelve miles from the closest neighbor or store."

"You've been there?"

"There's a good trout stream nearby." He grinned for the first time since he'd started the story.

"And you've fished it?"

Raised voices in the corridor kept me from hearing his answer.

Chapter Nineteen

I still want to speak with her," said Sarah Dodge. Sarah, a local defense attorney, is the first one I'd hire if I needed a lawyer. She's also a friend.

"It's not your choice, Sarah," the chief said. They were nearing the conference room. "Ms. Ryder doesn't want to talk with you."

"This is not a normal situation; you've got to take into account there's a child involved."

"You can talk with the prosecutor when he gets here, but you already know Lyle will tell you the same thing. Besides, Ryder hasn't asked about her daughter—only her dog team. Social Services is doing everything it can for the girl. They've kept her and the dogs together. They're letting her stay with Erin Donovan. It's the best situation possible."

"Being with her mother is the best situation possible," Sarah said.

"In your opinion."

"Do you have the AFIS report yet?" Sarah asked, referring to the automated fingerprint identification system.

"No," the chief said. "Why?"

Sarah didn't respond. They'd reached the conference room and she noticed Olsen and me.

The chief wore his standard-issue khaki pants and white shirt with muted tie. He stepped into the room, nodded to Olsen, and then looked my way.

"Vince, what are you doing here?" he asked. "How's Deb? Is there anything—"

"She's fine, considering."

"What about . . . ?" The chief left it hanging.

"What's wrong with Deb?" Sarah asked.

"Nothing," I said, lamely. Sarah would find out, but I just didn't want to get into it right now.

"You should be home," the chief said.

"I agree. But Deb kicked me out, said I was driving her nuts. By the way, thanks for sending a patrol car around."

"What is going on with Deb?" Sarah asked.

She stepped around the chief and set her monster-size briefcase on the table. Despite it being Saturday night, she was dressed for court as usual in a cream blouse and black slacks.

"Everything's fine," I answered. "Just find out who trashed our house, Chief. Freeman seems to think it's Deb's fault."

"Someone trashed your house?" Sarah interrupted.

"We're working on it, Vince," the chief said. "Go home. I've given all the news I can to either Mort or Holmes. I still can't believe Lou hired a retired funeral home director."

"Mortuary scientist," I said. "We prefer to call him Dr. Death."

"Whatever. Go home to Deb. Sorry to keep you waiting, Steve."

"Nice meeting you," Olsen said to me.

"Please call me when Lyle arrives," Sarah said to the chief.

The chief turned and left without confirming that he would. Olsen followed him out and Sarah turned to me.

"What's up with Deb?"

I started toward the door. "She wasn't feeling well yesterday. That and the fact that our house was trashed—we had a rough night."

Sarah walked with me to the lobby, grabbed her wool winter

coat and, after a few courtesy words with the desk officer and a nod toward Sunny D', who was sitting in the waiting room chair, we headed outside. As we passed through the door, I heard the officer tell Sunny that Freeman was ready. She was probably doing a report on snowmobile trail conditions or something.

Halfway through the parking lot, I asked, "Why'd you want to see Lupine Ryder?"

"Your co-worker called me."

I had to think about that for a moment, and then guessed, "Gina?"

Sarah nodded.

"She hired you to represent Lupine?"

"I didn't say that."

"I don't understand."

"Exactly," Sarah said.

Chapter Twenty

Back in the car, I called Deb.

"How's it going?"

"A couple students and teachers stopped by," she said. "Archie Freeman has been questioning them also. He suspects the kids are doing the trail vandalism."

"I'm not surprised. Just ignore him."

"I don't think so. Trying to stay above the fray just made me a punching bag for the hotheads. It's time to get proactive."

"Honey, I don't like the sound of that."

"You know the barricade someone put on the north trail? And the trees someone cut so they fell across the trail south of town? Freeman found leftover construction materials in the garage of one of my students and calls it evidence. He confiscated their father's chain saw, claiming he can match the sawdust in the chain to the trees cut over the trail. Can he really do that?"

"Not unless he had a court order."

"That's not what I meant. Can he really match sawdust particles?"

"A tree DNA test? Sounds a little far-fetched."

A thought crossed my mind as I told Deb that and I missed what she said next.

"I'm sorry. Could you repeat that?"

"I said the students are scared, Vince. Archie is intimidating."

"No doubt of that. But what if he's on the right track?"

"There's not a chance these kids are responsible. They're hopeless when it comes to this type of stuff. They'd be more likely to hack into the state's computer system and revoke snowmobile licenses or something. Building barricades, cutting down trees—it's just not their style."

"Yeah, I agree. So what's this proactive plan?"

"We're going to patrol the trails."

"You're out of your mind."

"Not me personally. I'm staying home. The teachers rounded up some parents and, along with the kids, they're going to watch areas of the trail. Tony is organizing them into shifts. In fact, once word of our plan got out, we've had plenty of people stepping up."

"Don't you think this is taking the civics class a little far, maybe crossing over into vigilantism?"

"We're not going to do anything stupid, Vince. We just want to help these kids out of a jam. And their parents are involved. How great is that?"

"You're staying at home, right?"

"Absolutely. I got that nice ham radio operator who came to the hospital last night to help. He's setting up a command center."

"I see." Visions of a junior Mort Maki invading my living room had my stomach churning. But I also knew this was Deb's outlet, and I was pleased to hear a little pep in her voice again. "Listen Deb, I'll be home in a little bit and, if it'll help, I'll take a turn on watch too."

I called Lou and was taken aback when Dr. Death told me Lou had stepped out for a bite to eat with Patrice Berklee. I don't know what kind of hold she had over him, but he hadn't eaten away from the office on a Saturday night since he'd owned the newspaper. Dr. Death said there wasn't anything new on the search for Earl Parsons. He then tried to tell me some story about a guy who wanted an obituary for his dog, but I cut him off. Let Lou deal with that.

I dialed Gina's number next. Still no answer, but I didn't expect one. I left her a message floating my strange idea, hoping it was enough to either spike her curiosity or get her angry enough to call me back.

Then, still sitting in the City Hall parking lot, I dialed Gord's cell phone.

"How's Deb?" were the first words out of his mouth.

I told him Deb had fainted without elaborating and then briefed him on her newly hatched scheme. It's better if the police know about it ahead of time.

"You two are unbelievable," he said. "Why can't she just kick back and watch some TV or do Facebook or something?"

"Freeman brought this on. Besides, I think they're organizing the patrols through Facebook."

"I know Archie rubs you the wrong way, but he's okay. Did you ever think that by alienating people the way he does that he gets people to slip up? It's not my preferred method, but sometimes it works."

"And sometimes innocent people get humiliated."

"Not innocent people, Vince—people who stick their noses in places where they shouldn't."

"If you say so. Anyway, the chief said you were waiting on the AFIS report for Lupine," I said. "Did it come in?"

Gord didn't answer.

"I'll bet you lunch at the Laughing Whitefish that I know what it says."

Gord sighed. "Vince, don't you have something else you need to be doing right now?"

I told him my hunch. He wouldn't confirm it, but Gord has

been my best friend since high school. It's a rare day when he can bluff me.

"It's on the chief's desk," he said. "I'll tell him you were asking about it."

"Tell him I'll be waiting for his call."

I hung up and called Deb again.

"Do you mind if I visit Gina before I join your stakeout?" I asked. "I'm kind of worried about her."

I explained what had been happening, and also my conversation with Gord.

"Are you serious?" she said. "I can't imagine what she's going through. Yes, you should check on her."

"Good luck at mission control," I said.

I spun my Bronco out of the City Hall parking lot and headed south toward Erin and Teej's farm, pretty sure that's where I'd find Gina.

Chapter Twenty-one

Erin and Teej live on an eighty-acre wooded parcel ten minutes south of Apostle Bay. A small part of their land is devoted to their log home and dog kennels. The remainder is a network of trails cut through jack pine and blueberry bushes.

The Donovans run their dog teams on the trails and offer guided tours as a side business, mostly to help pay for the dog food.

When I turned into their long driveway, a chorus of howls rose up. No one was going to sneak up to this place. I parked near Gina's pickup truck and walked a packed snow path past their porch and around to the dog yard.

Unlike most sled dog kennels, where the animals are chained to a center post with a swivel that gives them a ten-foot walk-around radius, Erin and Teej built individual dog yards, fenced by eight-foot-high welded wire. Huskies or German shorthairs paced back and forth inside the enclosed areas. A few came over to the fence and barked at me. Others slept in, or on top of, their doghouses.

Past the dog yard was a storage barn where Teej and Erin kept their sleds and gear, as well as snowmobiles and four-wheelers. Gina, Erin, and Bella, along with a fourth person, stood arguing in front of the barn.

Bella shut down when she saw me. Gina swore and walked away from the group. Lupine's dogs were anchored to a series of hooks along the pole building and the hackles went up on a few as I approached.

"Hi," I said.

Bella, wearing the same canvas overalls and cold-weather work gear I'd seen her in earlier, went to her dogs, dropped to one knee, and started whispering.

"Hi, Vince," Erin said.

"How's Teej?"

"Good. We brought the dogs in and got him a little food, but he's back out at Lake Margaret with the searchers."

The woman standing beside Erin looked cold and uncomfortable. I introduced myself.

"Mamie Richardson," the woman said, starting to take off her glove to shake hands.

"Keep your hands warm," I said. I looked over toward Gina to say hi, but she now had her back turned, and cigarette smoke rose over her shoulder.

"Mamie was going to put Bella up for the night—get her out of this cold and into a warm bed—"

"Over my dead body!" Bella shouted. "I'm not leaving the girls."

Erin sighed. "You've made that abundantly clear. I'm thinking none of us are going to sleep tonight anyway, so everyone can just stay here. You too, Vince. We'll make it a party."

"The dogs really need a run," Bella said.

"No, they don't, Bella," Erin answered. "They're still recovering from yesterday. We'll get them out for a little exercise in the morning."

"You don't know about real race dogs," Bella argued. "After racing, they need a run. It helps their recovery."

"A night of rest isn't going to hurt," Erin said. "We'll bring down a couple hay bales for their beds. Vince, give me a hand." I saw her wink at Mamie, and then she pointed toward the house, and I followed until we were out of earshot.

"Is Mamie with Social Services?" I asked.

"A foster parent. I offered to let Bella stay with me, but the sheriff said it had to be someone approved for foster care. The poor girl's having a hard enough time as it is, and the dogs are her only comfort. I think Mamie's just going to stay here.

"And Gina?"

"Not helping the situation."

"You know why, don't you?"

"She claims she's Bella's grandmother. It's absurd, isn't it?"

"I think it's true. Lupine Ryder is Amy Parsons—at least, that's what I think the cops aren't telling me."

"What they're *not* telling you? What do you mean?"

"A long story—the chief is buying time before he goes public."

We reached the far end of the yard, and Erin pulled back a tarp covering a head-high stack of straw bales.

"Take one of those back down to Bella's dogs," she told me. "Bella can spread it out."

I rolled a bale off the top, stuck a gloved hand under the string, and dragged it down the path. Erin pulled a second bale clear and covered the pile again.

The dogs growled at me when I drew near, so I swung the bale in front of me as a barrier and set it down.

"Here you go," I told Bella.

She ignored me, so I walked over to Gina, who took a final hit from her cigarette, doused the butt in the snow, and then put it in her pocket.

"Erin read me the riot act for flicking a butt onto the ground," she said. "Apparently the dogs eat 'em."

"Yeah, well, you know my opinion about smoking."

"I know, and guess what? I don't care. I haven't listened to any of your messages, but I can take a good guess what they say. Are you here on deadline?"

"No. I've been trying to find you."

"I'm not lost."

"You've helped me a lot over the last couple of years, Gina. I owe you."

"Then pay me back by butting out."

"When did you figure out Lupine was your daughter?"

"Who said she was?"

"Call it a lucky guess."

"The cops, I'll bet. She'd be in AFIS. I had to bail her out a few times."

"So, when did you know?"

"I wonder if subconsciously I knew when I saw her at the musher meeting. But it sure didn't cross my mind as a conscious thought. Amy was a little on the chunky side. She had long red hair and chipmunk cheeks. Lupine is like a skeleton with a crew cut. That black hair, and so gaunt—the only thing that's the same is the anger. She always had a monster-size chip on her shoulder."

"I should have figured it out when I talked to Earl a few days back," she said. "He smiled at me like he had some big secret. He must have known."

"Why'd you hire Sarah?"

"Tried to hire her, is more like it. She won't work for me. Is she blabbing about it already?"

"I saw her at City Hall," I said. "She's trying to represent your daughter."

"And that ticks me off. I want her to find a way to save Bella."

Gina lit another cigarette.

"Your truck was at Lake Margaret last night. I went down to the party to look for you."

"Maybe I didn't want to be found. You can be a prying jerk sometimes."

"Sorry. Any ideas why Amy returned to Apostle Bay?"

"Who knows why she ever does anything? Probably she

wanted to kick Earl's butt in the race or something equally stupid."

"She could have done that somewhere besides Apostle Bay."

"That wouldn't have the same kind of poetic justice for Amy's skewed way of thinking."

"Do you think she stole the cup?"

"Oh yeah, she'd have done that too. Why not take it before the race, save having to hang around afterward, would be her way of thinking. And she clearly deserved it."

"Get serious."

"I am."

"Then what about the bank robbery?" I asked.

"I've always thought Amy was the planner. Earl is a follower. Heck, Earl probably agreed to play along with her disappearance too, just to get rid of her once and for all."

Gina finished the cigarette and again doused it in the snow before pocketing the filter.

"How much of this is going to end up in tomorrow's edition?" she asked.

I shrugged. I still didn't know how I'd pull this off without a source.

"That Lupine is actually Amy. And that the cops are holding her as a suspect in the theft of the trophy."

"What about Bella?"

"She's a minor. We won't mention her by name. Lou will probably want more, but I don't have much to give him. And I still haven't been able to track you down, have I?"

Gina shrugged.

Erin joined us, leaving Bella to fine-tune the hay beds.

"I'm going inside to make sure Mamie's set," Erin said. "Do you two mind hanging out with Bella until I get back? She doesn't want to leave the dogs yet."

I checked my watch; it was almost ten.

"I wish I could, Erin, but I've got to run."

Erin's eyes pleaded with me to stay a few more minutes, but I owed Gina the time alone with Bella.

"Call me, Gina, if I can help you in any way," I said.

Then I took Erin by the arm before she could change her mind, and we walked up the path toward my Bronco.

Chapter Twenty-two

Once on the road again, I tried the chief, but he was out. I tried the state cops too, hoping for an update on the search for Earl, but the desk sergeant only took my number and promised to have someone call me back.

Then I tried Sarah's cell.

"Vince, is something wrong? Is it Deb?"

"No," I said, guilt dulling my enthusiasm. I'd call Deb next. "Deb's fine. I called on behalf of Gina. She could use your help and she really has Bella's interests at heart."

"Is that what Bella thinks?"

"The girl isn't old enough to know what's best."

"Really?" Sarah said. "So you're deciding for her?"

"Do you know who was sitting in that conference room with me at the police station?"

"I'm sure you're going to tell me."

"Steve Olsen, the FBI agent who investigated the bank robbery."

"So?"

"So Lupine/Amy, your quasi client, may be in jail for a while. Gina is next of kin. She can keep Bella out of foster care."

"How about this: if Lupine is Amy—we still don't know for sure—and if I can get her out on bail, Bella can be with her *mother*. And to go a step further, if Lupine is the woman who disappeared so many years ago, then she did it for a reason."

"Yeah, to skip town with the money."

"Or to get away from an abusive home life."

"Not according to Gina."

"Most abuse victims don't even get support from their parents, Vince. I know you think you're right on this, but you really don't know what you're talking about."

I called Deb next. She sounded better than she had in days— still tired, but focused and on a mission now that our home was the command center for what she was calling *Operation Snow-mo*.

It was a temporary lift, based on the distraction, but I was glad for it. I told her about my conversations with Gina and with Sarah Dodge.

"Be careful, Vince. Gina and Sarah are both friends of ours, and no good is going to come out of you pushing either one. Let them work this out on their own."

I knew she was right, but that hadn't stopped me from foolish acts before.

At the *Chronicle*, things were hopping. The weekend sportswriters were in their final hectic flurry of calls from local coaches reporting basketball and hockey results.

Mort, looking like a zombie with pasty skin and deep purple bruising around his eyes, still sat within his radio fortress. He wore the same jeans and gray, moth-eaten sweatshirt that he'd had on for two days. His unwashed hair stuck up in different directions like he'd been pulling it. I think the guy had been running for forty-eight hours on Mountain Dew Code Red.

"What's happening with the search for Earl Parsons?" I asked him.

"Huh, wha—"

"How's the search?"

"For Earl?"

"No, for the abominable snowman. Yes, for Earl."

"Nothing new since they found the hole in the ice," Mort said. "He's probably a popsicle by now. They've suspended the search until daylight."

"Then shut it down and go home," Lou called from his desk. "You look like one of Dr. Death's former clients."

"Yeah, sure, it's just . . ."

"What?" Lou asked.

"I've been listening to this weird chatter about something called Operation Snow-mo. Sounds like a vigilante group may be out patrolling the snowmobile trails."

Lou, pounding the keyboard at his desk, turned his basset hound eyes my way.

"Know anything about that?" he asked.

I was saved by my cell phone's chirp. Gord was calling.

"Hey, Bud," I answered.

"Are you near a TV?"

"Yeah, why?"

"Turn it to the news."

I waved at Lou, and then pointed to the TV mounted on the wall behind him.

"What's up?" I asked.

"You know what you asked me earlier, about fingerprints?" Gord said.

"Yes?"

"Lyle Simmons is going to release the information to Sunny D' in a moment. She's broadcasting live from our lobby."

Lou reached across his desk and grabbed the TV remote. He turned in his seat and flipped channels from CNN to the local news station.

"I suppose the competition is scooping us yet again," he grumbled.

Lyle Simmons is in way over his head, I thought, as I saw him standing next to the smiling weather geek. A first-year assistant prosecutor, he'd earned the title of chief law enforcement officer in the county when his boss, Rudy Clark, was elected to the Circuit Court as a write-in candidate. And that only happened because the sitting judge was murdered. Lyle hadn't even wanted the job, but he was Clark's flunky and the former prosecutor had engineered his appointment.

Simmons gave Sunny D' my story, and although Lou would be unhappy about it, I was glad someone else was breaking the news.

Chapter Twenty-three

The next morning, Sunday, Deb and I picked up Glory. Our little whippersnapper was apparently the only one of us to sleep well. She came bounding out of her grandmother's house, sans winter coat or hat, begging for a trip to the Laughing Whitefish. Our Sunday morning ritual was breakfast at the diner—a humongous sticky bun for Glory—then a visit with Missy Blue at Lake Superior Elder Care.

I'd tried to get Deb to stay home. Despite seeming invigorated Saturday evening, she'd crashed soon after I talked with her from Erin's house. She'd slipped between the sheets and let her Operation Snow-mo parents run things in our living room until I arrived.

I'd hardly slept, my mind constantly jumping from worries about Deb to Gina's dilemma to Earl's disappearance, which seemed awfully convenient.

Normally I'd have enjoyed breakfast at the diner, listening to the regulars gossip over news from that morning's paper, often news I'd helped report, or laughing at Glory's antics. Instead I was wishing we were at the doctor's office a day early as I watched Deb poke at a bowl of oatmeal.

Outside the diner, Apostle Bay was waking to a standard winter morning: gray, overcast, and windy. A few ice shanties sat on the frozen bay with fishermen hoping to land a whitefish or Coho salmon. The massive concrete and metal ore dock, silent for the season, seemed more a bastion of an industrial past than a mainstay of our economy. In a few months, when ore

boats returned and railcars moved along its length, we'd realize again why our founders had built this harbor town.

Glory was making a sticky mess of herself when a bright
yellow Hummer H2 pulled in front of our window, blocking
our view of the harbor.

Jack Reynolds Jr. climbed out, dressed as the typical high
school teen, baggy pants hanging several inches below his
plaid boxers, stocking cap pulled down over his eyebrows. His
father, in a slick leather coat and puffed up chest, came around
the vehicle's front and they both pushed through the café's
door.

The elder Reynolds scanned the crowd for anyone important he might need to impress. I looked into my coffee mug,
hoping the pompous jerk wouldn't come our way and force
me to act polite.

The race announcer and onetime mayor ordered his son to
sit at the counter and boomed out that the waitress should pre-
pare his usual. I sensed him moving toward our table and saw
Deb roll her eyes.

"What a crazy weekend," he said, stopping next to us, acting like we'd be glad of his presence. Deb glared at him.

"Jack," I said, hoping my tone would send him back to his
son.

"I guess you live for these types of weekends, don't you,
Vince?" Reynolds said. "Lots of great headlines mean lots of
papers sold."

I looked past him toward his son, who was now watching us.

"Spending the morning with your son, Jack?" It was my
hint that he should leave.

"Yes. In fact, I stopped by to let you know, Deb, and please
don't take this personally, but on Monday I'm going to with-
draw him from your civics class. Of course, you didn't intend
for things to get out of control, but now that it looks as if some

of his more overzealous classmates were behind the trail vandalism, I just can't—"

Deb, who had been ignoring him up to this moment, slapped her spoon down. I stood, interrupting before she blew her top.

"Jack, now's not the time for this."

"I've lost my appetite," Deb said. "Let's go."

"I just wanted you to know, Deb; it's nothing personal, just—"

Jack is the type who always steps into your personal space. And because he's big and buff, people usually step back. I haven't decided if it's intentional, or if he just doesn't get how rude it is. With my back against the booth, I had nowhere to step back to when he closed in.

"This is our family time, Jack. Why don't you hit the road?"

"Whoa, no need to get huffy," he said. "I can see why you're on edge, what with the school board meeting tomorrow to review Deb's class and see if things are out of control. I'm just—"

I'm not sure what was behind it, the lack of sleep, the guilt that I hadn't done enough to protect Deb, the burning desire to make Jack pay for dumping me in the harbor last year and leaving me to drown—probably a little bit of everything went into my shove. He toppled backward, crashing into a table, taking a plate of hotcakes and a mug of coffee to the floor with him. I momentarily enjoyed the elderly lady's shock as Jack landed by her feet in a clatter of silverware and broken glass.

Deb grabbed my arm. But she didn't need to. Beyond Jack, standing just inside the open door with a large grin on his face, was Detective Archie Freeman. Jack's son, still at the counter, had a smile on his face too, but for a different reason. He was evidently happy to see his dad go down.

Jack was back up in a moment, cream and syrup dripping

from his leather coat. He shoved a finger in my chest and stuttered, "Y-you'll pay for this."

He looked around the now silent restaurant and zeroed in on Freeman.

"Detective, did you see that? He assaulted me. There are plenty of witnesses. What are you going to do?"

Freeman sauntered toward me. He was in plainclothes, off duty, yet from somewhere he pulled out a pair of handcuffs.

"Oh, get real!" I said.

"By now, Marshall, you ought to know the drill," he said.

"And you ought to—"

"Vince," Deb cautioned, "don't make it worse."

"Ah, the voice of reason from your wife," Freeman said.

Reynolds was still spewing. "Did you see that? He assaulted me."

Glory stood in the booth, her sticky face beaming. She called out, "Hi, Speed Demon."

"Meet me at the station," I told Deb. I turned and walked past the cop, not giving him a chance to embarrass me further. "Let's go, Freeman."

I heard two things as I headed out the door. Reynolds exclaiming that I was a loose cannon—and a low but clear "That was cool" from Reynolds' son.

Chapter Twenty-four

Sometimes in the chief's office I feel like I'm back in elementary school, sitting before the principal, staring at my shoes and wishing I had the power to disappear. This was doubly embarrassing, having my family in tow.

I forced a smile, but it was lost on Glory, sitting in the chief's ancient wooden chair, spinning it back and forth like she owned the place. Deb, in an office chair that had long since lost its cushion, was deep in her own thoughts.

Not much had changed in the chief's realm since the days I tagged along with Dad on his weekly visits. The chief still used the same hard, green metal desk, and he still kept his records in dingy filing cabinets along one wall. He'd grudgingly accepted a computer, but even that sat on a side table and it wasn't turned on.

Recent additions to his decor were a photograph of sunflowers hanging on the wall and a calendar with songbirds. There was a new mug on the desk too, probably meant to replace an old stained coffee cup. It was stuffed with pencils. These were all signs of my mother's influence. She and Patrice Berklee seemed bent on softening curmudgeons with new ceramics.

The chief and Mom were now open with their dating, or friendly companionship, or whatever you'd call spending a lot of time together. They were even talking of a cruise together in the spring, something I'd never have guessed would appeal to either of them. I tried to picture them in Bermuda shorts or swimsuits relaxing in lounge chairs beside a pool. The chief's entry into the room killed that thought.

Glory stopped spinning. "Howdy, Chief," she said.

"Howdy, little flower," he said.

He circled behind Glory.

"Well, that's taken care of," he said.

Reaching past our daughter, he slid open a side drawer and reached inside.

"Here you go, Glory. A little treat courtesy of your grandma."

He pulled out a tin and pried the lid off, showing her some cookies. The chief wasn't the only one changing his habits under this new relationship. My mother had been on a baking binge since their romance bloomed, something she hadn't seen fit to do during my youth when a few batches of chocolate chip cookies or the occasional cake would have been greatly appreciated.

Glory studied the tin, searching for the largest cookie, and snagged one. She leaned back in the chair, put her feet up on the chief's desk, and chomped a bite.

"Glory, take your feet down," I said.

She ignored me.

"Vince," the chief said, with that tone I hate, "there have been times I've wanted to pop that smug—" He paused and looked at Glory. "Well, I'd think you'd have learned by now."

"But he was accusing Deb—"

"Correct me if I'm wrong, Deb, but you're a big girl now, right? You can handle it?"

"Last I checked," she answered.

"What if he'd been harassing Mom? And doing it in front of you?"

The chief chuckled. "Then God help him, because I think Loretta's tougher than the rest of us combined. Besides, Reynolds has a way of embarrassing himself if you give him enough time."

"I know. Sorry."

"What do you mean it's taken care of?" Deb asked.

"Let's just say I *explained* things to him, and he's seen fit to be magnanimous and forget anything happened—as long, of course, as Vince gives an apology."

"I'm not apologizing."

"Yes, you are," both the chief and Deb said at the same time.

I looked from one to the other and knew I'd lost that argument.

"How about the Laughing Whitefish?" Deb asked. "Any damages we need to pay for?"

The chief smiled. "Nah, they said it's good for business. But don't let it go to your head, Vince. You could really be in deep doo-doo here if I wasn't holding a few things over Reynolds."

"Thanks, Chief."

Glory was swinging the chair from side to side again. She'd grabbed another cookie. I stood to leave. "Well—"

"While I have you . . . ," the chief said.

I sat back down.

"Now, Deb, don't take this personally. I have to ask."

"Sure," Deb said. Her face was relaxed, but I noticed her fingers tighten on the chair's arms.

"Is there any chance, in your objective opinion, that one or maybe a small group of your students could be involved in the trail vandalism?"

Deb slid to the edge of her chair and started to answer, but stopped. She'd read the same thing into his question that I had: the chief had some reason to believe it was possible; he had some bit of information.

"I'm not saying you had anything to do with it," the chief continued. "Or that you're responsible in any way. I'm just asking, is it possible? Maybe they think they're doing the right thing. Maybe someone's being a little overzealous?"

She slid back in the chair. "Why do you ask?"

The chief considered his answer. Glory grabbed the cookie tin and held it his way. He took a cookie and told her thanks.

"Come here, Glory," I said.

"No," she answered.

"There might be a witness," the chief said.

"To the vandalism?" Deb asked.

The chief nodded. "We have someone who claims they saw two teenage boys near an area where trees were cut down to block the path. The person claims the boys were speeding away from the area on snowmobiles."

"This witness is sure it was teen boys?" I asked. "That's a tough call in winter with helmets, winter coats, et cetera."

"I know," the chief said. "We're just following up, that's all."

Glory popped at least half a cookie into her mouth and then, spitting crumbs, mumbled, "Can I get a drink, Papa?"

"Sure," I said. "C'mon, I'll take you."

"I can do it myself."

"No—" I said.

"Let her," Deb interrupted.

Glory shot me a self-satisfied look and then walked out the door, scuffing the heels of her boots on the floor in a way I knew was meant to annoy.

"What else?" Deb asked.

"The family of one of your students, a Jeff Hanson, they're building a barn near their house and they've reported some construction materials were stolen—lumber, nails, tools—stuff similar to what we found at the vandalism site."

The chief held up his hands as Deb started to protest.

"I know it's circumstantial," he said. "I also trust your

judgment. What do you think about Hanson, or maybe some of the kids he hangs around with?"

"He's a quiet boy. He's well-mannered. He doesn't draw attention to himself. I don't see him doing anything that would knowingly cause someone harm."

"You're sure?"

"I'm sure," she said. "I've actually thought about it, run through all the students, and I keep coming back to the belief that this vandalism is just not their style. These kids are creative, and some of them are supersmart. They'd be more likely to rewire an engine so it ran backward, or hack into the Chamber of Commerce's website and redraw the trail maps, something like that."

The chief nodded.

"One thing I'm pretty sure is that if the students are involved, word will get out," Deb continued. "High school kids can't keep secrets. I'll see some of them tonight and ask."

"During Operation Snow-mo?" he asked.

"Yes," she said. "You probably don't approve."

The chief shrugged. "Neighborhood Watch seems to work. This is similar—so far. I just hope it stays that way."

Deb stood. "I'd better go check on Glory."

I waited until she left. The chief dropped into his chair.

"Are you still holding Amy Parsons?" I asked.

He nodded. "But not for long, I think."

"Why?"

He contemplated his answer.

"We don't go to print until late tomorrow morning, Chief. It's not like I'm going to run back and write an article when I leave here."

"The trophy we found in her bag, the Superior Cup—it's a fake."

"A fake?"

"I had Perry check it last night. It's the right weight and size; the details are accurate. But it's not the trophy he made at his shop. It's not even real gold. Since that's the case, we can't very well say she stole it."

"Then why was she carrying it? I don't get it."

The chief shrugged. "Lupine Ryder, or Amy, isn't saying anything other than that she was set up."

"By who? And why?"

The chief shrugged.

"What about the bank robbery? Are you going to reopen that investigation? She was at least in the getaway car that day. She can explain what really happened."

"Except she's not talking. We're looking into it again, but I don't expect to learn much until Earl shows up, and that's looking less likely each day."

"Has Lupine even admitted that she's Amy Parsons?"

"No."

"Really? Even when confronted with the fingerprints?"

"Even then."

"Do you think she has something to do with Earl missing?"

"Vince, I don't know what to think at this moment, and you better not print that. Now, how are you and Deb holding up?"

"Fine. We've had enough other distractions to keep our mind off, well, you know . . ."

"In my opinion, you ought to keep your mind off the distractions and on what's more important."

Chapter Twenty-five

I found Deb and Glory in the main lobby. Glory was sitting in a chair next to the dispatch operator, talking into a spare, unattached microphone. It brought back my childhood and the times my father and the chief left me with the dispatcher, a roly-poly guy named Nick who I thought was Santa Claus in his off-season job. Nick taught me how to handle callers who believed their next-door neighbors were Communists spying on them, and he taught me how to play the card game *Speed*. I grew to recognize his regular callers' voices and could recite their complaints word-for-word: a neighbor's leaves were blowing into their yard, those dang kids were riding bikes too fast, and some punks are driving their car with loud rock-and-roll music blaring.

Nick would always wink at me, while in a sincere voice he'd commiserate with them over the decline of society. Looking back, it was probably these times I spent with Nick that spurred my first purchase of a police scanner, and maybe even my career in journalism.

Deb coaxed Glory away from the mic and into her winter gear. With our daughter clasping both our hands and skipping, we headed toward the exit where Sarah Dodge stood, stomping snow off her feet.

Sarah hugged Deb and shot me an angry glance.

"Deb, how are you?"

"Between Vince making a fool of himself, and the people in

this town who take their snowmobiling a little too seriously, I haven't had a chance to worry about how I am these days."

Sarah glared at me again. "Yeah, well, I haven't had any run-ins with snowmobile people, but I can say your husband's not on my A-list these days either."

I lifted my hands in surrender. "Seems to be the general consensus."

"Daddy got 'rested again," Glory said.

Sarah cut short whatever snarky comment she'd been about to throw my way and said, "Huh?"

"Just a little misunderstanding with Jack Reynolds," I said. "That's all."

"He had a fight and fighting's not nice," Glory said.

"Glory, that's not exactly—"

"That's exactly what happened," Deb said.

"Jack and you?" Sarah asked.

"Look, it was a minor disagreement, that's all. Jack was being his usual self—"

"Listen to what you're saying," Deb said. "Jack was being his *usual self.* It's nothing new. You've got to learn to ignore his jabs before it really costs you."

"Yeah, I get it already."

"Did you assault him?" Sarah asked.

"Yeah, salt and pepper and even oatmeal went flying," Glory said.

"She's exaggerating."

"No, she's not," Deb said.

"Well, at least I didn't require your services, Sarah. It's all cleared up."

"Except the mess on the lady's coat," Glory said.

Sarah finally cracked a smile, which I promptly ruined.

"How's Bella?" I asked.

"How do you think?"

"At least she'll be back with her mother soon."

"What's that supposed to mean?" Sarah said.

"Talk with the chief. I think he has some news you'll like."

Despite my protest that Deb needed rest, we headed next to Lakeview Elder Care for our weekly Sunday visit with Missy Blue.

Glory and I had met the grande dame of Lakeview two years ago when I'd brought her along on assignment to interview a resident. Glory had been mid-meltdown as we entered the lobby, and Missy saved me loads of embarrassment, first with a cookie and a tissue, and later by entertaining my little sprite.

The two of them developed a friendship that grew into weekly tea parties in the common room. However, Missy's health took a downturn this fall. Now we meet in her room.

Missy has always treated Glory like a grandchild, Deb like a queen, and me like a pain in the rear who is necessary but barely tolerated. It's all part of her act.

We found Missy propped up in bed watching a local Finnish-language TV show that runs every Sunday.

"Sorry we're a little bit late," Deb said.

"I'm not surprised," Missy answered. "He's with you."

"Papa 'salted some mean guy," Glory said. She climbed onto Missy's bed, the only bed she didn't treat as a trampoline, and handed her friend the dark chocolate candy bar we'd brought. "Here, it's good for you. Mama says if you eat some every day, you won't have accidents."

Missy frowned.

"Glory, dear, I said it has antioxidants."

"Okay, then you won't have no oxidants," Glory said.

"Thank you," Missy answered. "There's something for you on the dresser, dear. Why don't you get it?"

Glory climbed from the bed and retrieved two small tissue-paper packages.

"Both for me?" she asked.

"One's for your mother," Missy answered. She reached over and took Deb's hand. "And how are you doing?"

"I'm fine," Deb said.

"I'm sorry about what happened. It's not your fault, you know. So don't let yourself think that way."

"Huh?" Deb said. She looked at me. I shrugged. I certainly hadn't said anything about Deb's condition.

Missy studied us, then said, "Hard as it seems, these things happen for good reasons. Next time everything will work out fine."

If there is a next time, I thought.

Glory climbed back onto Missy's bed, handed Deb one package and, unlike at home where Glory would shred the tissue wrapping like a demon, she carefully peeled back the taped edges. She slid out a bright silk scarf with yellow daisies.

"It's beautiful," she said and looped it around her neck.

"You shouldn't have," Deb said, as she pulled out a matching scarf.

Their joy was mirrored on Missy's face and, like every week when we visited, I was glad we made the time.

While Deb and Glory modeled their scarves, I fell back into Missy's armchair and rested my eyes. I must have drifted off, because my chirping cell phone woke me.

"Vince, you know those things mess with people's pacemakers," Missy said. "Every time Roberta's daughter visits, she forgets to turn hers off, and the next thing you know, Ralph down in room 108 has heart palpitations, although I think it might actually be from watching that exercise channel. All those tarts jumping around in their underwear—it's just shameful."

I fumbled in my pocket and silenced the ringer. I didn't recognize the number on the screen.

"Sorry, Missy. I forgot."

"Obviously," she said.

I saw I'd interrupted some kind of girl talk by waking up.

"I think I could use a cup of coffee or an energy drink. Anyone else want something? I'll make a trip down to the cafeteria."

"I don't think they have energy drinks there," Deb said.

"Well, they ought to. It would get this place rocking."

"We all know you're going out to answer that phone, Mr. Important News Reporter," Missy said.

Missy was right, of course. I went down to the lobby where a pot was always brewing and poured myself a cup, tossing a dollar into the donation jar. I made a mental note to put this place on the same anonymous coffee donation plan as the cop shop. Cup in hand, I went to the empty waiting room, a place I'd become familiar with on my many visits with Glory, and dropped into an ocher-colored chair. I pulled out my phone, but returned it when I saw Deb round the reception desk and head my way.

"That wasn't much of a girls' chat."

"Missy sent me out to talk with you. She thinks we need alone time."

"She said that?"

"No, but it's what she meant."

"Have a seat," I said, waving my hand across the room. "Wasn't that creepy the way she knew about the miscarriage? It's like the time last year I was covering the cemetery vandalism story and she said I smelled like death. Do you think she really has some kind of sixth sense?"

"Nothing would surprise me with Missy."

"Me either."

"What do you think she meant about next time?"

Deb shrugged. "Do you think there should be a next time?"

I shrugged.

"We'd have to change our lifestyle," she said.

"Change our lifestyle, or move away from here."

"You know what I remember most about living in Grand Rapids?" Deb said. "We weren't under the small-town microscope all the time. I mean, not only does everyone know our business here, but they think it's part of their business."

"On the other hand, people look out for each other here too," I said.

"For example?"

"How about the way people came together last night to patrol the trails? Or the way this community stood up against building luxury condos in Explorer's Park last year?"

"Those same people open the newspaper to the courts page and revel in a neighbor's embarrassment. It makes them feel superior."

"Yeah. So, are we talking about leaving town again?" I asked. "Or are we talking about having another child?"

"I don't know," Deb said. "Sometimes I love it here in Apostle Bay. And sometimes I want to start over, to go someplace where no one knows me, where no one trashes our house, where people don't call you at all hours of the day and night."

Once again Deb looked defeated, and I knew it was beyond the strain of the miscarriage and the snowmobile harassment. The life was draining out of my feisty, fun-loving, dedicated wife. She was too depressed to even cry.

"Then let's go, Deb. Anywhere you want."

"It's not that easy."

"Sure it is. You name the place. We pack up and go. It'll take a little time to work out the details, but truly, we could be out of here by summer."

"Somewhere warm?"

"Anywhere. We can pick the place and look for jobs when we get there. We've barely touched that money we inherited. We can live off it for a while and find what we want. Who knows, maybe I can even stay home, write cheesy, bodice-ripping romance novels and care for Glory and . . . and her brother or sister."

"Would you like that?" she asked.

"Writing cheesy romances? Probably not. But that isn't the point. I'd find something."

"What about Loretta?"

"Mom's fine. She has the chief. He'll retire soon. They'll hit the cruise ship circuit."

"But—"

"Deb, this isn't working for us. I understand that."

She nodded. I moved to the chair next to her, took her hand, and wondered, if we did move, would that really change things?

Back in Missy's room, Glory played with the dolls that Missy kept for her. Missy's eyes were closed, but she opened them when we entered.

"It looks like you've worn out Missy," I said. "Let's pack up and get you home, little girl."

Glory whined and sounded like she was ready to launch into an argument, but a stern look from Missy stopped it.

"Gosh, I wish I could do that," I said.

"If you gave her a little warning, instead of just showing up and telling her it's time to leave, you probably could," Missy said.

"As always, you are right."

"Don't forget it," she said. Despite the frown she aimed at me, I glimpsed humor in her eyes.

Deb helped Glory put the dolls back on Missy's dresser.

My two girls arranged their matching scarves and thanked Missy again. She dismissed them, but told me to stay behind a moment.

"Why don't you two go out and warm up the car?" I suggested, wondering what I'd be lectured about now.

"I saw last night's news, and it helped me figure something out—something I've wondered about all these years," Missy said.

"What was that?"

"Amy Parsons has a daughter. She's about fourteen?"

"Yes."

Missy nodded. "I was in the bank that morning."

"No way," I said. "During the robbery?"

"Of course I was there during the robbery. Why else would I be telling you? I'd found an error on my bank statement and went to get it corrected. I was sitting in the little waiting area across from the tellers. A nice young girl who didn't have a clue what she was doing was trying to help me. Poor girl, I think it was her first month on the job, and when that gun went off, she fainted dead away."

"What did you do?"

"I watched the whole thing, of course. I told the police Earl Parsons didn't do it, but they wouldn't believe me. The fools had already decided it was him, and nothing was going to change their minds, especially an old biddy."

"If the old biddy was you, they should have listened."

"Exactly," she said, "because everyone else in that bank acted like a bunch of hysterical ninnies. You'd think they'd be used to gunshots with all the hunting we have around here."

"Okay," I asked, "how do you know it wasn't Earl?"

"The person behind that mask was pregnant. And I highly doubt that Earl was pregnant."

I pictured Missy telling this to Steve Olsen and the chief.

The two grizzled veterans probably sent her out the door and rolled their eyes as she left.

"And, um, you've always had this ability to sense pregnancies?"

"Of course," she said. "Anyone can if they pay attention. I figure it must have been Amy Parsons who robbed that bank. Her daughter is the right age."

"Don't you think other people could tell if it was a man or a woman, from the voice or the physical stature?"

"Yes, if they hadn't had their heads buried somewhere, afraid of being shot."

I made a mental note to get the original witness interviews from Gord and read them myself.

"It's not going to be easy tomorrow," Missy said. "You understand what I'm saying, don't you?"

"Yeah, I do, Missy. You're talking about Deb's doctor appointment."

"Right," she said. "Please be on time next week."

Missy leaned back on her pillow and shut her eyes. I watched her for a final moment and shook my head in wonder.

Chapter Twenty-six

When we got home, there were several messages on our machine, all for Deb, and all about setting up that night's patrol of the snowmobile trails. The most ominous of these was Ray Varvil's brusque, "Please call me back."

Varvil is the school superintendent. He's been quick to judge Deb in the past—and slow to apologize when he was wrong.

"He's probably suspending the class," she said.

"Who cares? You're going to take a few sick days anyway. In fact, why not cancel the trail patrols for tonight and rest up for tomorrow?"

"I can't. Things are already set up. And not only are the students fired up, their parents are. When you've got parents willing to help, take advantage of it."

I considered arguing and realized resistance was futile. "Okay, go to it. Glory and I'll whip together a late lunch."

Deb walked back to our bedroom to work the phone. I really wasn't sure what she hoped to accomplish, but understood that sometimes just taking action felt good. Meanwhile, Glory and I decided to make chocolate chip pancakes. Deb came back moments later to find our daughter standing on a chair at the counter stirring batter and wolfing down chocolate pieces, while I emptied the dishwasher.

"You're never going to believe what Varvil wants," she said.

"That's easy. He's insisting you stop the trail patrols, says it's a liability for students and for the school district."

"The opposite," she said. "He wants to help."

"You're right. I don't believe it."

"It's true. He said the reputation of our students and the reputation of our school are on the line and he wants to participate."

"More likely he wants to observe and find another reason to say you're doing something wrong," I said.

"Possibly, but he admitted I've always come through on the right side in the past. Maybe he's giving me the benefit of the doubt."

"Um, that's great. Or maybe he sees political advantage to this."

"I had a call from Thomas Holmes too," Deb said. "What do you think that's about?"

"Whoops, I'd meant to tell you: he's been assigned to cover the story of your little vigilante group. Lou wanted your buddy Mort on it, but the poor guy ran screaming from the building when he heard about your involvement."

Glory jumped off her stool.

"Like this," she yelled. Raising her hands overhead, she ran shrieking out of the kitchen, into the living room and back again.

I nabbed Glory on her pass by the kitchen table and spun her around.

"Just like that," I said.

"If he writes about our patrols, the vandals are sure not to come out," she said. "They'll know we're watching."

"Is your goal to catch someone in the act? Or ensure the trail is safe?"

"It's both."

"Maybe the publicity will be good. Otherwise, your volunteers are going to lose interest in a few days. Actually, maybe Varvil caught wind of Holmes' interest and that's why he wants to tag along."

Deb went off to make a few more calls. Glory helped me set the table so we could have—in her words—breakfast for lunch.

Chapter Twenty-seven

I let Deb and Glory sleep in the next morning when I left for work. Operation Snow-mo had been uneventful, but we were all wiped out by the late night.

At City Hall, Gail Stevens buzzed me through security and handed me a copy of the dispatch log. A quick scan showed there was nothing of consequence other than the search for Earl Parsons—that was being handled by the state cops now. There were also a couple of reports of loud noise, a stray cat howling at a house, and someone requesting assistance because he'd locked his keys in his car.

Gail told me that the cross-country ski conditions were great the past weekend and that I really ought to take up the sport. She'd probably skied thirty or forty miles over the weekend, a light jaunt for her. In my mind it was way too much work to be considered fun.

I slipped down the hallway to Gord's office and declined his offer of coffee.

"I'm on a tight deadline," I said. "I just stopped by to see what you could tell me about Lupine's—I mean Amy's—release."

"She's over at the county jail, so it'll probably be as soon as the administrative staff gets in," he said.

"And Perry Iverson is sure she didn't have the real gold cup?"

Gord rolled his eyes and I realized it was a dumb question. He'd probably triple-checked it with Perry.

119

"You still want to look at the bank robbery file?" he asked.

"Absolutely. I'll be back this afternoon."

"Steve Olsen's going through it now in the conference room if you want to check it out with him."

"I wish I could, but I'm scrambling to make this morning's deadline as it is. How about this afternoon?"

"Whatever works," Gord said. "The case hasn't moved for fourteen years, I don't see much changing with that. I just wish we had a way to keep Amy Parsons around for a few more days."

"You can't hold her for . . . ?"

"For what? No, we can't just hold her. Although I think Steve's desperately trying to find some reason that we could."

I thought about poking my head into the conference room to check with Olsen, but decided I'd better get cracking on my story for the morning.

I left City Hall and detoured two blocks west to the county jail on the off chance I could find Amy's release time. The deputy on duty told me it was up to the court. I tried the prosecutor's cell phone, but no luck.

From the county building I hoofed it across the street, through the small park to the *Chronicle*'s rear entrance. I entered the loading dock door, nodded to the pressmen who were just starting their shift, and headed upstairs to the editorial bull pen.

Gina sat behind her desk, hammering her keyboard, and that surprised me. I'd expected her to be AWOL again considering Lupine's impending release.

She looked refreshed, not the worn, cigarette-smoking character I'd seen the day before. I wondered if she'd finally connected with Bella, but didn't dare ask.

Lou was grumbling over his computer, either scanning the

daily wire for anything we needed or, more likely, pondering that day's op-ed piece. The sports guys were arguing about something to do with the Red Wings' game over the weekend.

Holmes sat erect at his desk, dressed in his usual mortuary attire of dark suit, starched white collar, and perfectly knotted, blue-with-a-subdued-pattern tie. He was entering the daily obituaries and, as always, I couldn't help watching the precise way his fingers poised over the keys and tapped each with an even pressure while the rest of his body remained primly straight.

I dropped into my desk chair and checked Lou's ubiquitous sticky notes that usually decorated my monitor or phone. One reminded me to follow up on Amy Parsons, a no-brainer; the other directed me to check with the cops on the Earl Parsons search since Mort Maki was at the musher banquet this morning.

I called central dispatch and left a message for the lieutenant spearheading the search, and then checked my messages, expecting the typical whack jobs complaining about a story I'd written. I had two messages; both were hang-ups.

Lou called our morning editorial meeting to order as I replaced the receiver.

"All right," he groused. "After getting scooped over the weekend on the Amy Parsons reincarnation and arrest, and having some of our people missing"—he looked directly at Gina when he said this, and she stared him down with an equally fierce expression—"I want to know how we're going to recover today."

This was Lou's usual Monday complaint, and I no longer made the effort to point out that because the TV news was Saturday night, while our paper didn't come out until Sunday morning, we were scooped every weekend. Besides, our newsstand sales probably improved when the television news broke a story.

"Gina," he said. "You first."

"I don't have anything for today," she replied, and I heard the challenge in her voice. Reporters never say they don't have a story, because if you do, you get a lecture and then get assigned to some crummy piece.

I leaned back, ready to watch the battle of wills. Instead, Lou just nodded. "I understand. Why don't you take care of the briefs then?" he said, referring to short news pieces that we used on inside pages. "And then, if you're due some time off, take it."

Okay, I thought, *this green tea diet thing must really be working.*

"Vince, what have you got?"

"Nothing from overnight dispatch," I said. "The cops did find an ice fisherman passed out in his shanty on the bay. He'd had a bit too much to drink and it looks like that cost him a few toes."

"Uh, right," Lou said. "What have you got on the Amy Parsons/Lupine Ryder thing?"

"Amy is going to be released this morning," I said, watching Gina for her reaction. "All charges are dropped."

"What?" shouted Gina.

"It turns out the trophy found in her bag, the Superior Cup, was a fake. The cops don't have any reason to hold her, although I know they wish they could."

"But—I don't understand," Gina said. "They can't just let her go."

"Am I missing something here?" Lou asked. "I thought she was your daughter."

Gina ignored him. I knew what concerned her. Amy was going to skip town and take Bella. Gina might never see her granddaughter again.

"I can't believe this," Gina said. "Why didn't you tell me?"

"I thought you knew."

Gina bent down, yanked open her bottom desk drawer, and grabbed her purse. Then she kicked the drawer closed and took off.

"Wait," Lou called. "Where are you going?"

Gina didn't bother to answer.

"Great," Lou said. "Care to enlighten me?" he asked.

I explained about Bella. He shook his head.

"I feel her pain," Holmes said.

"Huh?"

"Nothing," he said.

"Okay, so where are you at with the story?" Lou asked.

"I still have to talk with Perry Iverson, and I've got messages in to the prosecutor. Don't sweat it. I've got it covered. Can we send the photog over to try and snap a picture of her leaving the jail?"

"Skip it. We'll use a photo from the race start Friday, and Patrice is going to pull an old picture for me this morning from when Amy Parsons went missing."

"I don't understand something," Holmes said. "If she had a fake trophy, why didn't she just point that out and save herself from being arrested in the first place? Why deny she knew anything about it?"

"The only reason I can see is if she thought she had the real thing. Gordon Greenleaf said it is a very good fake. I guess it had the right weight, details, et cetera."

"Then that means—"

"Either someone planted the fake trophy in her bag, wanting everyone to believe she stole it—"

"—or she stole a fake in the first place from Iverson's," Holmes said.

"Except why would Perry have a fake in his store?"

"A display model?" Holmes suggested.

"But he'd have known it was the fake stolen, and he'd still have the real one, so that rules that out. I've been wondering if Earl Parsons stole the trophy and then planted the fake on Amy. Not only to expose her real identity, but also to give him time to get away with the real gold trophy after the race."

"I'd think it would be easier just to win the race and tell everyone she was Amy Parsons," Lou said.

"I keep thinking back to the start," I said, "when Lupine's—Amy's—dogs got loose. It was chaos. Glory got caught in the middle of it. That would have been the perfect distraction to plant something in Lupine's sled bag."

Lou shook his head. "I just don't see someone going through all that."

"I've been wondering about something else," I said. "Lupine tore through the Dahinda checkpoint on a mission to catch Earl in the race. The next thing we know, he's missing. Coincidence?"

"Didn't you mention she was a suspect in his disappearance?" Holmes asked.

"Gordon said he floated the idea as a way to keep Amy in town, but no one took it seriously. Especially now that the searchers believe Earl went through the ice. Has Mort learned anything else about that?"

"We'll know in about an hour. He went straight to the musher breakfast this morning. Apparently, instead of the usual awards ceremony, they're turning it into kind of a memorial service."

I picked up my phone and started to dial central dispatch again.

"What if they're working together?" Holmes asked.

"Who?" I asked.

"Earl steals the gold trophy and disappears. Amy shows up with a fake, knowing the cops can't hold her, but it delays them while Earl gets farther away."

"Yeah, except how does he get farther away? His sled and dog team were found. He'd have to be on foot in the middle of the wilderness."

"They stage the accident. Amy Parsons gives him a ride until he's close to a town where they've prearranged with someone to meet him."

"I don't think so. Under that plan, Amy had to know she'd be discovered. She was reckless coming here, but I don't believe she planned for anyone, other than maybe Earl, to discover her identity. It would obviously open up the whole bank robbery thing again. I just don't see it."

"Maybe it's not the first time they've worked together," Holmes said.

"You mean the bank job?"

"Why not?"

"Everything I've heard is that they didn't get along."

"What you heard or think doesn't matter," Lou said. "What are the cops saying? What's Amy saying? That's what matters. You've got a deadline. Get cracking."

I had even less time if I was to make Deb's appointment. While Holmes talked about the snowmobile surveillance, I dialed the city cops and asked for Gord.

Chapter Twenty-eight

Gord laughed at the idea of Amy and Earl Parsons working together to steal the gold cup.

"There's no way they could have planned something that elaborate without Earl's handler having an idea. And Jon Bishop, unless he's an amazing actor, is genuinely upset that Parsons is missing. He blames himself."

"Why?"

"Earl was sick all Friday, Bishop said. Real sick with some kind of stomach bug. They decided to switch places Friday afternoon because Earl was in no shape to drive the team."

"So what happened in Dahinda?"

"According to Bishop, Earl recognized his wife at the start. And he couldn't take the thought of losing to her. He insisted on taking over in Dahinda. Bishop said he couldn't talk Earl out of it. However, because Earl was still sick, Bishop thinks that he either passed out, or he wasn't thinking clearly, and he let the dogs run off course, getting lost in the storm. He said they weren't using their most experienced lead dog and that might have contributed to it. I think it's plausible."

Gord had little else to add. I looked up the number for Perry's Gold Rush and started to call when my cell buzzed. The caller ID showed SARAH DODGE.

"No," she said.

"No what? You called me."

"No, Lupine is not talking with you. No, we don't have any comment other than it was unconscionable that the police

126

held my client for as long as they did and we're considering action. And no, I won't speculate on any other unfounded rumors."

"So she's officially your client now?"

"Yes."

"What about Bella?" I asked.

"It's also unconscionable that mother and daughter have been kept apart for so long. You can print that."

"I mean, what about Bella and Gina and Lupine working something out?"

"That's their business," Sarah said.

"I'm not asking as a reporter. I'm asking as Gina's friend. I'm worried about her."

"Why? Gina's not planning anything stupid, is she?" Sarah asked.

"Not that I'm aware. I just wish they could work something out, that's all."

"We don't know all the circumstances, Vince. There could be a very good reason why Lupine Ryder has no interest in pursuing a relationship with Gina. You of all people should know this."

Ouch, that stung. I tend to forget I once had similar feelings.

Sarah ended the call. I dialed Perry Iverson. No answer at either his home or shop, so I left a message. Certain that he'd dodge me, I decided to try and catch him in person.

"Lou," I said. "I can't get Perry on the phone. I'm running across the street to see if he's in his shop."

"Don't be long," he growled. "I've only got Holmes on the desk this morning, and he's actually supposed to be doing his obits, not reporting. And while you're out, swing by the historical society and grab that photo from Patrice."

Outside, it was snowing again, nothing major, but enough so that the sidewalks were covered and a few store owners were shoveling. I jogged across the street and down the two blocks to Iverson's Gold Rush. The front door was locked, but I could see light beneath the heavy velvet drapes at the back of the showroom.

Perry didn't answer when I banged on the door, so I went around to the back alley and pounded on his rear entrance. Then I tried the handle. It turned easily, so I pushed it open, thinking it odd that Iverson hadn't locked the door, considering he'd been robbed only two days ago.

I walked through a small storage area lit with fluorescent lamps. Metal shelving lined the walls, holding cardboard boxes of various shapes and sizes. A thick layer of dust covered most of the stuff. Off to the right was a rest room, with the door partway open, so I could see the sink, commode, and a medicine cabinet.

The room was maybe eight feet deep, with a wooden door at the end leading into Perry's workshop. I knocked on the door and pushed it open at the same time.

Perry jerked away from his desk, spilling coffee out of his mug and across his arm. He gasped, dropped the mug onto his desk, and then shook the liquid off his hand. A half-eaten dough-nut sat near his mouse pad.

"Sorry to startle you," I said. "I knocked, but the door was open."

He reached forward with his dry hand and turned off the monitor, waving his other hand like it was on fire. Then he spun in his chair and grabbed a rag from the worktable behind him.

His bench held an array of files and screwdrivers and little things that looked like dentist picks. Two magnifying lenses mounted on long arms rose like preying mantises off the table.

There were also small, propane gas canisters and a torch.

Beyond the workbench I noticed the backside of the maroon, velvet curtain separating the showroom from his work area.

"I'm not open yet," he said.

Round, 70s-style glasses made his eyes bug out. His brown hair was long, thinning, and looked in need of washing. Creases radiated from his eyes, the result of a lifetime spent squinting at small things. Perry was skinny and every movement seemed herky-jerky, nervous.

"Your front door was locked, but I saw there was a light on back here, so I came around hoping I'd catch you. Sorry to barge in. Don't you think you should lock it, you know, after the robbery?"

"Yes, I should lock it," he said peevishly. He made a point of blowing on his hand and then wiping it again. "I must have forgotten to this morning. What do you want with me?"

"Your expertise. The cops told me about the fake trophy, the one found in Amy Parsons' sled bag. They said you're the one who examined it. I'm writing about it for today's edition and I need a few more details."

"I don't think I should comment."

That's pretty much what everyone tells me when I first approach them. I've learned it usually means, *I want to comment but not be held responsible for what I say.*

"In your professional opinion, how good was the fake?" I asked. "I mean, it wouldn't take a perfect replica to fool a couple of volunteer race officials out in Potlach."

"You want my professional opinion?"

"That's why I'm here. You made the original, so I figure you're the expert on this."

"That's right. . . . Uh, well . . . I mean, I did make it. Uh, not the fake. I didn't mean that. I mean the real one. So I'd know a fake."

"Like I said, that's why I came to you. How good was the fake?"

Perry continued wiping his hands and then running the rag along his desk, although the coffee was by now gone. His eyes bounced around to every place in the room except where I stood.

"Oh, it was very good—quality work—hard to tell unless you are an expert."

"Why?"

"Why what?"

"Why would it take an expert? What made it so hard to detect that it was not the real thing?"

"The weight, for one thing," Perry said. He rolled his chair over to a set of shelves behind him, turning his back to me and sorting through some boxes. "And the attention to detail. It was a perfect match to the original."

"So it probably took a professional, a jeweler like you, to make it?"

He spun around and, for the first time, his bulging eyes met mine.

"Oh, no, I didn't make it."

"I didn't say that you did. I meant it would take a person with your skills."

"Yeah, I guess so."

He turned back to the box and riffled through the contents. I glanced at the shelves that were filled with open shoe boxes. Each was labeled in black marker with what I assumed was a project or client name.

"Found it," he said. He spun back toward me with a manila folder full of papers and laid it on his worktable. Flipping open the folder, he pulled out sketches of the Superior Cup.

"How would another jeweler know about the fine details

on the cup?" I asked. "I mean, very few people saw the finished product."

"These," he said, pointing to the sketches. "The sled dog race committee has to approve my design each year before I make it. Actually, I think it's the Grey family who has to approve it. They're the ones paying for the thing and they're very particular."

"The design is different each year?" I asked.

"Of course." He sounded offended. "Each one is unique. That's part of the attraction. Once they approve the design—and let me tell you, usually they wait until the last minute; this year I didn't get it until the week after Christmas—anyway, once they approve it, they write a check, and I can buy the gold and start the work."

I made a mental note to ask Gord if the cops were running down who else had the sketches.

"You have to buy the gold?"

"You think I keep twenty-five grand worth of gold lying around here?"

I looked around his shop again and wondered how he stayed in business, even with the novelty factor. I'd heard about Perry buying the cup back each year from the winning musher for a huge discount and wondered if that was part of his business plan.

"Perry, what did you do with last year's cup?"

"Huh?" He started shuffling the sketches and returning them to the folder, but the sheets kept falling the wrong way. Finally he just closed the folder, mashing the sketches, and returned it to the shelf.

"Last year's cup?" I asked again. "I heard you bought it from the musher after the race. Is that true?"

He laughed a lame laugh and, with his back toward me, kept fiddling with the box.

"Bought it from the winner?" he asked.

"Yes."

"Nope, didn't happen," he said.

"It makes sense to me," I said. "What would a musher do with the cup? Most of them live in log cabins. They don't have large trophy cases, but they do have travel expenses and dog food bills. And you could put the gold to good use in your jewelry. It's a win-win."

He gave me a direct gaze for only the second time in our conversation.

"I know that rumor goes around," he said, "but why don't you find last year's winner and ask him. Go ahead." He started with the rag again. "Gold prices were skyrocketing, and that trophy is worth about twenty-five percent more now than it was a year ago."

"So that means this year's trophy would be about twenty-five percent smaller in size? Am I right?"

"Yeah, something like that. Look, I, uh, I've got finish working on my accounts and get the shop open."

I glanced at my watch. It was 7:45. He didn't open until nine, but I wasn't getting any more from him. I harassed him into letting me take a mug shot, saying it would be good for his business, and then left through the back door.

Outside the shop I called Mort's cell phone. I left a message that while he was still at the musher breakfast, he should track down last year's winner and ask, preferably in a casual way, if the cup had been sold back to Perry.

After that, I walked to the Historical Society, arriving in the back alley as Patrice Berklee climbed out of her car.

"I suppose Lou sent you," she said, slinging a large bag over her shoulder.

"What, I can't just stop by to visit my favorite archivist?"

"You never do unless you need something," she said.

I followed her through the back door, into the main lobby of the former bank building, through the large vault door and then into her office.

"By the way," I said, "whatever magic you are working on Lou, please keep it up. The guy's actually tolerable now when things don't go right."

She waved a hand as if it was nothing. "A simple change of diet," she said.

She slipped out of her black coat, and underneath I noticed a sapphire blue scarf draped over one shoulder of her black blouse. I had to bite back a comment about it being the first time I'd seen her wear any color besides black. I used to joke that, as a historian, she was mourning the present. Maybe the relationship with Lou was affecting her too.

Patrice walked behind her desk, pulled open a drawer, and took out a CD. She handed it to me.

"What's this?"

"The photos Lou wanted."

"On disk?" I said, dumbfounded. Although Patrice was all for state-of-the-art preservation practices, she'd been a little late entering the computer age.

"I tried to e-mail it, but I haven't got that attachment thing worked out yet."

"You? E-mailing?"

"Ha-ha," she said. "Although you may think I'm learning this stuff to make your job easier, I'm not. Now that I can scan and save documents and photos, I can let people like you have copies instead of worrying you might damage original things. Of course, there's a charge with it."

"I thought our deal was that the *Chronicle* gets stuff free since we donated all of our archives to the Historical Society."

Our previous owner, while bankrupting the newspaper and

alienating everyone in town, also decided to clean house. He gave the Historical Society our entire morgue. In the long run, it turned out to be for the best. Patrice cataloged everything and now has all the past issues stored properly, rather than piled in the back of a dusty closet.

"You can use the material for free," she said. "You have to pay the standard fee for data transfer."

I didn't have time to argue.

"Okay, bill it to Lou."

"Cash only," she said.

"Get out."

"I'm serious. We must treat everyone equally. That will be five dollars."

Knowing I had another favor to ask, I dug out my wallet and gave her five wrinkled ones. She took the money with a look of distaste.

"Thanks for the disk," I said and turned to go.

"Wait for your receipt."

"Sorry, Patrice, I'm on deadline. But I'll be back this afternoon to look at everything you have on the big bank heist of fourteen years ago. Any chance you might pull the files together for me by lunchtime?"

"I'm very busy with—"

"It'll be worth it when I give you the story behind everything."

She sighed. It was the one thing she couldn't resist, a story that had something to do with Apostle Bay's past.

Chapter Twenty-nine

Back at the *Chronicle,* the usual deadline chaos reigned. Mort, frazzled and looking like he hadn't slept since the last time I'd seen him, was hunched over his keyboard, banging out a story on the musher breakfast. He looked ready to snap, so I didn't bother him about the Superior Cup.

Lou had left a hospital press release on my desk about some new wellness program they were starting. He'd circled a sentence that said the hospital staff was "facilitating a partnering relationship to better utilize" something or other. He'd scribbled "rewrite" in the margin.

First I added some comments from Perry Iverson to my story. I also put in a blurb about Sarah considering reparations from the police for holding her client. I checked with the prosecutor's office to make sure there were no changes, and then filed the story and cranked out a rewritten version of the hospital piece.

At eleven, Lou sent down the final page, and I slipped out the back door and headed over to Deb's OB/GYN office for her appointment.

I found Deb in the waiting room, slumped in a chair, hiding her face in a magazine. I slipped into the seat beside her and squeezed her hand. We were surrounded by enthusiastic women in various visible states of pregnancy, all babbling about their upcoming parenthood.

Deb gave me a wan little smile and the receptionist called our names. I got the feeling they'd just been waiting for me to arrive.

The nurse settled us in, checked Deb's vitals, and asked her a series of questions. She explained that what had happened to Deb was common and told us not to worry.

Then she left the room.

"Getting tired of everyone telling you this is normal?" I asked Deb.

"A little."

"How do you really feel?"

"Other than all the emotions swirling around inside my head, I think I feel . . . normal."

We were laughing when the doc, a woman ten years our senior with sharp features and gray-streaked frizzy hair, entered. She looked up from the chart in her hand.

"Laughter is good," she said. "Is this nervous laughter, or are you doing okay?"

"A little bit of both," Deb said.

I hadn't seen this doc since Glory's birth, but Deb had been in for annual visits and liked the woman's no-nonsense manner. She answered our questions about Deb's health and the possibility of future children and, while I stepped briefly away, she examined Deb.

When I returned, the doc had softened her clinical bedside style and was asking about Glory's development.

"Call me," she told Deb. "I mean it." She then turned to me. "Make sure she does. I want to hear Deb's voice in a week. Even if it's just to tell me about your little girl, understand?"

"I promise," I said.

Deb and I had a half hour before it was time to pick up Glory at preschool, so we grabbed two coffees and drove down to Benoit Beach.

Waves crashed onto the shoreline ice-shelf, a jumble of fresh ice and broken chunks stained brown with sand. The average temperature this winter had remained mild and the bay wasn't frozen solid as it is most years. That's probably why we'd had the extra snow lately—more warm moisture in the air, rising and creating what Sunny D' and her cohorts would call lake effect snow.

"Are you really feeling okay?" I asked.

"Just tired, I think."

"Thought any more about what we talked about yesterday?"

"You mean moving, or a sibling for Glory?"

"Both."

"That's all I have been thinking about."

"Come to any conclusions?"

"How about you? Have *you* come to any conclusions?"

"I just want what makes you happy."

"What if I said the same thing? Where would that get us?"

"In an endless loop, I guess."

"Right. We have to figure out what we're both committed to; otherwise we'll both go nuts. It's like when you decided to work part time at the paper and you ended up working more than full time. You weren't committed to the change. Same as when I took maternity leave and then got on the bargaining council."

"Don't remind me."

"We need to examine what's really important to us, and then build our decision around that. We can't be impulsive because we're tired or things seem out of control."

"You're more important to me than anything," I said. "You and Glory."

"That may be," Deb said. "But we're not all you need."

"It *may* be? What do I have to do—"

"Vince, I know you love me," she interrupted. "I'm just saying that we have to think about a lot of things before we make any life-changing decisions. Our careers are part of who we are. And they should be part of our decision. Do you agree?"

"Sure. You're saying that the added chaos of another child at this time wouldn't be a good idea."

"No, I'm thinking the opposite."

"You'd prefer life to get crazier than it is?"

"No, I think life would get better in the long run if Glory had a brother or a sister."

"Really?"

"I've also been thinking that when she's older, having a sibling, someone she can lean on in times of need, might be a good thing. It's something you and I, being only children, never had."

I thought back to when I'd been going through the mess with my mother and learning about my adoption. I wasn't sure if it would have been any easier having a brother or sister.

"Not all brothers and sisters are best friends," I said.

"But they are family," she answered.

"Are you thinking we should try again?"

"I do miss having a baby," she said. "Glory's getting so independent. And she'll be in school soon."

"We'll have more freedom when that happens."

"You think? There will be piano lessons and dance and sports and after-school activities and you name it."

"And having another child . . . ?"

"Will make it crazier, I know. But we'll make it work, don't you think?"

"We always do," I said, because I was pretty sure that's what she wanted to hear.

I dropped Deb back at her car outside the OB/GYN office. Her plan was to get Glory from preschool and they'd spend Deb's free afternoon doing mother/daughter stuff.

The sun was making a halfhearted attempt to burn through the slate gray ceiling overhead. I took it easy on the winding county road that led to the Donovans' kennel. A mile from their place, I came upon a truck parked against one bank, nearly blocking the road.

When I drew close enough, I saw it was the Nightshade Kennels pickup. Rubbing the right bank with my tires, I inched even with the driver's window and looked inside at an empty cab.

I rolled down my window and caught a whiff of overheated metal and burned oil. It came from Lupine's truck, as did the sound of whining dogs. I edged forward and saw wet dog noses poking out the breathing holes in their boxes. Some dogs started growling. Not wanting to stir them up, I continued forward.

Ahead, Teej's truck came around a bend and slowed. I pulled as far to the right as possible and stopped. Teej pulled alongside and rolled down his window. Erin and Bella sat inside the cab with him.

"What's happening, Teej?"

"A little engine trouble," he said. "I'm going to tow her back up the road to our place."

Bella wasn't crying, but seemed about as close to it as possible. Erin had an arm over her shoulders.

"How's Deb?" Erin asked.

"Good," I said. "We just left the doctor's office and got the thumbs-up. She'll be fine."

"Great," Erin said. "Tell her we've been thinking about her."

Just like Erin, I thought, *a major crisis unfolding at her home and she's asking about the well-being of someone else.*

"I will. You guys need some help?"

"I think they need more help back at the house," Teej said. "We can handle this."

I gave him a quizzical look. Bella kept staring straight ahead.

"Why don't you pull ahead?" he asked. "Give me some room to climb out of this bucket."

I pulled forward. Teej got out of his truck and walked up to my window.

"Gina and Amy are having a knock-down-drag-out brawl back there," he said. "Sarah is trying to referee, but I think they just need to get it out, you know, clear the air. That's why we took Bella with us, to keep her out of it."

"What happened to the truck?"

"There's a huge puddle of oil and a drain plug in our drive-way where it used to be parked. I figure someone didn't want Amy or Bella going anywhere."

"Gina?" I asked.

"That would be my guess. Sarah said the truck drove fine on the way here."

"Great."

"We'll take our time, if you know what I mean. How about you go on up to the house and make sure one of them girls doesn't end up with an assault charge, or worse."

"Thanks for giving me the easy job," I said.

"You want to stay and explain it all to Bella instead?" he asked. "She's a good kid. I hate to see all this raining down on her."

"Yeah, me too. I'll head up to the house. What's the latest on the search for Earl?"

"The cops say they aren't going to find him until spring."

"Really?"

"They think he's either buried under a foot of snow or, more likely, at the bottom of the lake."

"And you? What's your thought?"

"It doesn't seem real. Earl knows how to take care of him-self. But I guess he was sick, so maybe he pushed his luck after all. It's a shame."

I watched Teej walk back to his truck and decided my prob-lems seemed small compared to what Gina, Bella, and Amy were going through.

Chapter Thirty

I parked next to Gina's blue pickup. Ahead, Sarah stood on the Donovans' front porch, leaning against the railing, bundled in her down coat, stocking cap and gloves. She glanced at me, shook her head as if I were just one more problem headed her way, and then returned her gaze to the kennel area.

I could hear the dogs howling and, above that, the argument. Gina's angry voice rang clear, as did the harsher, curse-laden words of Lupine.

Black oil had melted a patch of snow on the driveway and a thin drip line headed out toward the road. Teej had been right; Lupine's engine was toast. I understood why Gina may have done it, but I would probably have found some less drastic way.

The verbal battle raged, and from my perspective, neither woman was listening to the other. It had evolved to name-calling by the time I joined Sarah.

"Sounds like quite the reunion," I quipped.

She shot me a dirty look.

"It had to happen sometime," I said. And then, when she didn't respond, "Have they been going at it long?"

"If one word of it shows up in the newspaper, I'll—"

"Whoa, Sarah. I'm here because I owe Gina some big-time support. I don't know how, or if I can help, but I'm here."

"Well, she's gone off the deep end," Sarah said, and nodded toward the driveway. "That act of vandalism could land her in jail."

"Do you blame her?"

Beyond us, there was a lull in the shouting. We both leaned over the railing toward where the women were arguing and caught another earful. They'd just been catching their breath.

Sarah sighed.

"Yes, I do blame her," she said. "She had no right."

My cell phone rang. I reached into my coat pocket and silenced it.

"Why did Amy come back to Apostle Bay?" I asked. "Do you think that maybe, on some subconscious level, she wanted Gina to know she had a granddaughter? I mean, why risk everything?"

Sarah shrugged. "Who knows? Amy probably doesn't even understand why she returned."

I was thinking the opposite. Amy returned for a specific reason, but things have spun out of her control.

The voices down by the kennel had dropped enough that we could still hear them going at it, but the shouting lacked volume. The dogs dropped their voices too, only the occasional yip punctuating the air.

"Well, I guess she and Gina have a few more days to figure it all out. I'm sure the cops won't be too bummed she's sticking around either."

"What's that supposed to mean?" Sarah asked.

"C'mon, Sarah. There are a ton of questions about what really happened fourteen years ago. I talked with a witness just yesterday who, back when the bank robbery had just happened, said it was Amy behind the mask, not Earl Parsons. The cops wrote her off at the time, but maybe they shouldn't have."

"That's absurd," Sarah said. "Earl was a wife-beating, misogynistic—"

"That's what people once believed. I think the police are reevaluating that theory now that Amy has returned."

"Don't you dare defend him!" Sarah shouted. "It always

works that way: the victim becomes the one who did wrong; the abuser is treated like a victim. People make excuses: the woman deserved it, she was too hard to live with, she needed to be put in her place. Physical violence against someone is a crime, Vince. And as far as I'm concerned, Lupine Ryder was justified in doing anything necessary to get out of her situation, including faking her death."

"I'm not defending spouse abuse, I'm just—"

"You *are* defending it." She pointed her gloved hand at me. "I thought you were different, but you're like everyone else."

That last bit stung. I tried to remind myself that it was Sarah's past talking. Deb hinted it had been horrendous. Sadly, it was blinding her now, and I feared Amy was taking advantage of it, though I had no idea how to convince Sarah of that.

Sarah stomped off the porch and headed toward Gina and Amy, probably ready to now channel her anger at Gina. That would only make things worse. Any compromise between Gina and her daughter was going to need Sarah's support.

A moment later, Gina came running up the hill toward her truck.

"Gina, wait," I shouted, stepping off the porch to intercept her. I caught up as she was pulling her vehicle's door open. She kept her back to me, and at first I thought she was breathing hard from running, but then I realized she was sobbing. I put a hand on her shoulder. She twisted away. I stepped back and gave her a little space, but not enough so she could ditch me. I had no idea what to say, so I tried a little humor.

"I'm not sure who was howling louder, you two women or the dogs."

No response. She took a deep breath and composed herself, and then climbed into the driver's seat. I held the door open.

"Don't go yet."

"Go?" she snorted. "I'm not going anywhere."

She reached across to her glove compartment and I feared the worst. Seeing her grab a pack of cigarettes was, sadly, a relief. With a trembling hand she lit one.

"No, sir," she said. "I don't plan to let her out of my sight."

I was about to ask about the truck vandalism, or the fight, but realized I'd be beating a dead issue.

"Well, that will work until Sarah gets a restraining order. Then what are you going to do?"

She turned toward me and I saw her right eye was red and swollen shut. She'd been popped and was going to have a shiner.

"Prove that she robbed that bank," she said. "Or at least that she was in on it. Because right now, that's the only way I know to save my granddaughter."

Chapter Thirty-one

I took off when Teej, Erin, and Bella returned with Lupine's truck. There was enough turmoil at the kennel that they didn't need me adding to it. Erin announced she was leaving also, taking Bella into town to pick up canine supplies.

Back on the main road to Apostle Bay I remembered the phone call I'd silenced while talking with Sarah. I pulled over to check the message, and heard a terse "Call me back." I didn't recognize the number, but dialed it back, hoping it wasn't one of the weekly crackpot calls I get from the newspaper job.

"Who's this?" a woman's voice answered. At least it sounded like a woman.

"Vince Marshall. You called me a little while ago and left a pleasant message that I should return your call."

There was dead air and I thought the connection had been lost.

"Hello?" I asked.

"Yeah."

"Um, can I help you with anything?"

"You're the guy who wrote that story about Amy Parsons?"

"That would be me."

"You want to know what really happened with that bank robbery, and how Amy disappeared?"

"Of course I do."

"Then meet me at Hart's. Nine tonight."

"Who is this?" I asked.

"That's not important."

"Look, I get these kinds of calls all the time and most of them don't pan out," I said. "I'm not schlepping out to some bar tonight for a clandestine meeting. If you really have information, you ought to call the police."

"I can't do that."

"Listen, I appreciate the call, but—"

"I can't talk to the cops because I was there. I was part of it."

"Part of what?"

"Everything," the woman said. "You want to know more, be at Hart's."

"But how will I—"

I was speaking to dead air.

I called Gord next and offered to bring him lunch when I came to browse the bank robbery file. As usual, he declined, not wanting to take favors from an old school chum.

I gave him the number from my anonymous caller, explaining her claim. He said he'd look it up before I got there.

Next I called Deb to see how things were with her and Glory. They were shopping for spring clothes. Deb sounded happier. Just being away from work and home was probably helping.

I checked in with Lou after that and gave him a brief rundown on Gina.

"You've got to cut her some slack, Lou. This whole situation has knocked her for a loop."

"Understandably," he said. "I'd tell her to take some time off—*if* she ever called in."

"Is Mort around?"

"Gone to lunch," Lou said.

"I heard the sheriff's wrapping up the search for Earl Parsons."

"It looks like the scavengers will be the first to find him now," Lou agreed.

I made a quick spin by a fast-food drive-in and then headed to my appointment with Gord.

At City Hall, Gail buzzed me in, looked disapprovingly at my lunch bag—she's lectured me on multiple occasions about my diet—and told me I'd find Gord waiting in his office. On the way I passed Freeman in the hall. He grunted a greeting. I nodded back, figuring the fewer words between us the better.

Gord was tapping at his keyboard. He waved me to a seat when I knocked on his door frame.

"Hey, bud," I said. "I brought an extra burger. Sure I can't talk you into it?"

He rolled his eyes. "There's Missy Blue's interview," he said, pointing to a photocopied statement on the corner of his desk.

"What about the other files?" I asked.

"Spread out in the conference room. Steve Olsen's moved in."

"I see. Any chance I'll get to look at them without filing a Freedom of Information Act request?"

"Sure. Olsen said to send you on down."

"Wow, I'm not used to this type of cooperation from my local law enforcement pals."

"Don't push your luck," he said.

Gord finished typing and then leaned back in his chair. He dressed more like the chief each day—khakis, white shirt, blue tie—and I wondered if he was subconsciously prepping for the role once the chief retired. My godfather had been making noises about it lately.

"Any luck with that number I gave you?"

"Yep."

"And . . . ?"

"It belongs to Rowena Marchforth. She lives north of town."

"The name doesn't ring a bell."

"She happens to be the person who discovered Amy's clothing in the pit toilet, back when we believed she'd been murdered."

"What do you think of her claim? You know, that she was involved in the robbery."

"Hard to say. But Olsen lit up when I mentioned it to him."

"Why'd you tell him?"

"Because that guy's got this entire case cataloged and filed in his brain. I'm still playing catch-up."

"Don't you think it's strange the way he's kept tabs on this robbery all these years? He even told me he'd spied on Earl Parsons in Minnesota. And now what—he's coming out of retirement?"

"If you were in his shoes, what would you do?" Gord asked.

"Move to Florida and play golf or something."

"Right. You'd be doing the same thing. I feel sorry for any young reporter at the newspaper about twenty years from now, having to deal with your crotchety old self. Heck, you'll probably come in just as often after you retire as you do now."

I didn't like that picture. It got me thinking again about my conversation with Deb and where we were headed. Gord interrupted the thought.

"Did you hear me?"

"Sorry, I was picturing my crotchety old self coming in to share a cup of coffee with some wrinkly old police chief."

"We want you to meet her tonight."

"We? Who's we?"

"Olsen and me."

"Why don't you give her a visit? Better yet, haul her in and give her the old good guy/bad guy routine."

Gord reached forward, lifted the photocopied report I had requested, and waved it from side to side.

"Cause maybe we're reevaluating this witness statement in light of new information."

"She's going to enjoy saying 'I told you so.'"

"Don't get ahead of yourself," Gord said. "We're only re-evaluating."

"Right," I said, happy in the thought that someone else would be the target of Missy's scorn.

Chapter Thirty-two

Olsen gave me marching orders on how to interrogate Rowena. He wanted me to wear a wire, but I laughed and explained that it would be the end of my journalism career if people in town found out I was a police snitch. Deb and I might leave town, but I'd rather it be our choice, not a consequence of my poor judgment.

The chief was conspicuously absent from our meeting, and that had me wondering if he didn't know what was going on, or if it was his way of saying he didn't like the idea.

Olsen told me that Rowena Marchforth and Amy Parsons were friends in high school. During his investigation, Rowena gave detailed accounts of Earl's abuse of Amy. Rowena also claimed that Amy stayed at her home, using it as a refuge when Earl got out of control.

Rowena's testimony was the primary reason the cops thought Earl murdered his wife.

As Olsen told me this, I started wondering if Earl and Amy Parsons were still officially married. Was Amy now Earl's heir?

Back then, Rowena had been a custodian at the hospital. She'd been on disability for the last several years. She still lived north of town, a few miles from where Earl and Amy Parsons had their former kennel. Rowena never married and had no kids. Olsen didn't have much else for me.

At home that night, Deb wasn't pleased about me going back out, especially since she'd planned to do the vigilante thing again, despite her doc's orders. Thankfully many of the volunteers had backed out for the night, citing Sunny D's prediction of subzero temps. I suspected they were really making sure Deb took the night off. By now, most of them knew what had occurred.

I assured Deb that vandals usually weren't the type willing to freeze their tootsies off, and also that the risk of her students suffering frostbite wasn't worth it either. I left her and Glory snuggled up to a video and hot cider.

I parked at Hart's about ten minutes early, zipped my coat up to my chin to shut out the bitter wind, and climbed out. The stars were bright in the sky. When there isn't a blanket of cloud cover over Apostle Bay, nighttime temperatures dip below finger-numbing cold.

Hart's is a small building, not much bigger than a thirty-by-thirty brick square with a neon sign glowing OPEN. A brown door was centered in the building with a window on each side. I knew from seeing the place during the daytime that the windows were either darkly tinted or blacked out.

I jogged to the entrance. Inside, a fried-food haze seemed to permeate the air. Hart's was a bar from another era and so was its clientele, mostly retiree blue-collar workers who didn't have anywhere else to be on a Monday night. The place needed fresh paint and a thorough cleaning. Instead the owners had installed dimmer bulbs in the lamps, hoping to hide the decay.

Three guys sat together at the bar, talking with the female bartender, who looked to be the oldest of the group. None of them acted like they noticed I'd walked in. A few empty stools separated them from a gray-haired man who sat nursing a brown bottle. I caught his face in the mirror behind the bar. He looked away.

The rest of the place was empty. I picked a square table in

the middle of the room and sat, facing the door. The waitress/
bartender made no move to acknowledge my presence.

I glanced again at the old man, but he was now engrossed
in the Red Wings game.

I felt Rowena arrive—it was probably the cold air as she
opened the door. Encased in a ratty fur coat that seemed so
familiar, she popped her bare hands out of the long sleeves and
pulled off the hood, squinting, as if the dim lights had blinded
her. Rowena's graying, wiry hair was pulled back tightly from
her forehead. She paused, more likely to catch her breath than
search for me, and then she stepped to my table.

She slipped out of her threadbare coat, hung it on the chair
opposite me, and then sat close. She was diminutive, almost
malnourished, it seemed, not healthy, not aging well.

"I figured you'd show up," she said, her voice hoarse either
from the cold or from smoking.

The bartender or waitress or whatever she was arrived at
the same time with a glass that looked like it had cola in it.
She set it on the table. Rowena grunted thanks.

"Better bring me a second, hon, and he's paying."

"Sure thing, Ro." The waitress eyed me for the first time, and
then asked, like it really pained her, "How about you? Want
anything?"

"A Coke will be fine, thanks."

The lady snorted and walked away.

Rowena Marchforth studied me with an intensity that made
me feel uncomfortable.

"I suppose you're going to say I don't look like my father," I
said.

"Don't know what he looks like," she said. "But you look
okay. Not my type, but okay."

"I'm glad you think so."

"What, that you're not my type?"

"No, that you think I'm okay. It's nice to meet you, Rowena Marchforth."

"Well, gee, you're not as stupid as you sounded on the phone," she said. "Can I assume you also know my connection to Amy Parsons and we can skip the small talk?"

The waitress returned with my drink. "Twenty bucks," she said.

"Ha-ha," I said.

She stuck out her hand. I stared at it for a moment, but couldn't outlast her and didn't want to be here all night. I dug out my wallet. All I had were some ones and two twenties. I peeled out a twenty.

"They charge that amount when you're paying?" I asked Rowena.

The waitress snickered and left us. I lifted my glass to drink, caught a whiff of something that didn't register until the burn hit my mouth, and I spat the drink back into the glass. There was way more whiskey than Coke in the drink.

"Tsk-tsk," Rowena said. "A waste of good spirits."

"I wanted plain soda."

Rowena laughed. "Marge doesn't serve that here."

"Marge doesn't have much business either."

Rowena shrugged. "You may have figured out my name, but you can't use it in your newspaper."

"Huh?"

She leaned closer and said, "Just in case you've got a wire or tape recorder or something, I'm just saying right now that everything I'm telling you is all made up. You clear on that?"

"A wire? Get real. You want to frisk me or something?"

"I already told you, you aren't my type."

She killed her drink in two big gulps, and set the glass gently down next to the one I'd spit into.

"I'm not sure what you want from me, but let me assure

you, I don't record conversations secretly." *Very often,* I added to myself. "And I also don't use anonymous sources in news stories. It's a big no-no with my boss."

"I knew this wouldn't work," she mumbled.

I shrugged and sat tight. She studied the table. Over at the bar, all four patrons were watching us in the mirror now, and the bartender stared directly at me.

"I'm not going to jail," Rowena said.

"Why would you?"

"I won't."

"I'm not in the habit of arresting people."

She fired me a dirty look, saying this was hard enough as it was. I decided I'd better keep my mouth shut if I wanted to get anything out of this.

"Amy robbed that bank."

"And you know this . . . how?"

"Because I helped her. And I helped fake her death so she could get away from this place."

"I see. And you did this . . . why?"

"Ain't that the million-dollar question I've been asking myself for a whole bunch of years now?"

I heard the hitch in her voice, which she tried to mask by grabbing my drink and taking a slug.

Since Marge was staring at us, I didn't need to get her attention. I just pointed at Rowena's empty glass. The bartender sighed, as if I'd interrupted something other than her being a busybody, and brought Rowena another glass. She left the empties on the table. I handed her my other twenty, not expecting change.

Rowena lifted the glass and gulped.

"Why don't you tell me how she did it," I suggested, specifically not saying how *you* did it.

"The bank job?" she asked.

"Sure."

"Amy had it all planned out. We went while Earl was out training the dogs; that way he wouldn't have an alibi. She dressed up in his clothes and put on a ski mask to hide her face. She had me dress like her, wear a wig 'cause of her red hair. We took his truck. All I had to do was sit in the truck, make sure people saw me. I had to look like I was captured or something. Amy tied this rope around my wrists; it was loose, but nobody outside could tell if I held my arms up briefly. And she gagged me, but it was my own bandanna. I just had to look all forlorn and stuff, but not too soon, only as we were driving away. It would've screwed things up if someone tried saving me while she was inside robbing the bank."

"Yeah, I can see that," I said.

"So, I didn't have anything to do with robbing the bank. I was just Amy's alibi."

Rowena fished a cigarette out of her coat pocket and ran it through her fingers.

"Dang new smoking laws—not even in bars, for cripes' sakes."

"Why'd you help Amy? Why even take the chance?"

"Oh, there wasn't much risk. Like Amy said when she was planning the whole thing, if someone caught us, I was just a captive. I could say she forced me to do it. I wouldn't have. Not back then. But I could have, so it wasn't much of a risk really. She was the one taking the big chance."

Not in the eyes of the law, I knew. But it probably wouldn't be wise to tell her that.

"So what exactly happened?" I asked. "You stayed with the truck. Amy went inside. And then what?"

"She fired off a couple shots into the ceiling, using that gun she stole from her mom." Rowena paused, a memory coming to mind. She laughed. "Amy used to bring that gun out to a field where we'd hang out after school. We'd smoke a few Js and she'd shoot the dang thing off. Scared the bejesus out of me a time or two, and I swear, one time Twitch pissed his shorts."

"Who?"

"Nobody. Anyway, I guess they gave her the dough and she came running out, jumped in the truck, and we drove off. She made sure to hit a few cars on the way out of town. Not enough to slow us down, just enough to make sure everyone knew it was Earl's truck. I held up my hands and tried to look like a captive; although I was laughing behind the gag so hard tears came out. I read in the paper some people thought I was crying. Ha."

She downed the drink. I was out of twenties so didn't wave for another.

"Then what happened? Did you two split the money or what?"

She snorted.

"No, Amy took off with it. I stayed behind, pretended to find her clothes in that pit toilet out by Eagle's Rock park. Made up a big story about how Earl had been abusing her, whipping her within an inch of her life, locking her in closets, yada, yada, blah, blah."

"He wasn't?"

"Earl? C'mon. If he'd put a hand on Amy, she'd have laid him out flat."

"I see. From what I can tell, most people believed you."

"Yeah, except Earl's alibi royally screwed things up."

She reached for the glass, realized it was empty, so she picked up the cigarette and started fiddling with it again.

"You still haven't answered why you did it. Just being a good friend?"

"It's not important now." She waved her glass toward the bar. I knew everyone in the bar was watching us and wasn't surprised when the woman arrived a moment later with another glass, her gnarled hands setting it on the table.

"Put it on my tab," I said, cutting off her request for more cash. I waited for her to leave and then asked Rowena, "Why should I believe anything you've just told me? Even if I did believe it, what do you want me to do with it?"

"I really don't care if you believe me or not," she said.

"Then why this meeting? Just wanted to get it off your chest?"

"Because she double-crossed me, okay?" she hissed. "Because she was supposed to send for me once she got away and set us up with new identities and a new place to live. All these years I wondered, what the heck happened? Did something go wrong? Was she afraid to contact me because Earl got off? She left me hanging. And then she comes strolling back to town and doesn't so much as look me up or explain what happened."

"She used you," I said.

"Oh yeah, big time," Rowena said. "And what did I get for it?"

"It looks like a big chip on your shoulder."

"You could say that."

"Why didn't you ever come forward?"

She glared at me like it was the stupidest thing she'd ever heard.

"I know you don't want to go to jail," I said. "So what do you expect me to do? Write about it? Say I met some anonymous person in a dimly lit bar who claims this?"

She shook her head.

"Don't do a dang thing . . . I just thought someone should know."

Chapter Thirty-three

About halfway home I noticed a white SUV on my tail. When it followed me off the main road and then into my driveway, I figured it was Olsen. I closed my eyes and wished the guy away.

"So, what did she have to say?" he asked me. He wore no hat or gloves and walked close up to me as I climbed from my vehicle. He probably expected me to invite him inside, but it wasn't going to happen.

"Can't this wait until tomorrow morning?" I said, shutting my Bronco's door and slapping my hands together for warmth.

"Not if Amy Parsons is planning to leave town and you have information that will stop her."

"Amy's not going anywhere. Her truck is out of commission."

"I'd like a little insurance, just in case," he said.

I wasn't sure what he meant by that. There wasn't anything he could do. I just wanted him gone.

"Here's the short version. Rowena Marchforth claims that she and Amy robbed the bank, and they framed Earl for it. They also set up Amy's death. The plan was for Amy to skip town with the money and send for Rowena when the heat died down."

"But Amy never did," Olsen finished.

"Right."

"So Rowena's ticked off that Amy came waltzing back into town."

"Something like that. The problem for you and me is that Rowena's not willing to go public. Listen, I'm freezing here, and no offense, but I know my wife and I aren't up for visitors tonight, so I'll give you the rest in the morning."

"Yeah, I understand," he said. "In the morning."

"At City Hall?" I asked.

"Sure," he said.

For some reason, the smile he flashed me before turning away disturbed me. Maybe it was relief at finally knowing what happened, but I couldn't get it out of my head the rest of the night.

Chapter Thirty-four

Gail buzzed me through security the next morning, handed me a copy of the overnight dispatch log, and told me Gord was waiting in his office. Her cheeks still showed red chilblains, probably from her morning run or ski or whatever endurance training she'd done before work.

I still hadn't decided how much I should tell Lou about my meeting with Rowena, or how I could possibly use it for deadline that day. Maybe Gina could shed a little insight—at least tell me if Rowena's claim was possible.

Halfway down the linoleum corridor, I heard Olsen's voice behind me.

"Vince, wait up."

I turned and let him catch me.

"It's been like forever since I last saw you," I said, with as much sarcasm as I could muster.

"Follow me," he said. He took me by the bicep and pulled me down the hall, like a little kid tugging their parent toward an important discovery.

"What's going on?"

"Bear with me; I want to show you something."

"Okay," I said, realizing it would be faster to comply than argue.

He steered me back toward the conference room, where I thought we were headed, but we kept going, heading toward the chief's office. Halfway there he stopped and turned toward me, getting a little too close for comfort.

"So let me get this straight," he said. "Rowena Marchforth told you she participated and helped plan the bank robbery with Amy Parsons?"

"Yeah, that's the gist, but—"

"And she and Amy framed Earl?"

"That's what she said. Listen, can't we—"

A slam and a loud curse came from the small conference room a few feet beyond us. I'd just been set up.

Marchforth came out of the door calling me several names that I'm glad my daughter didn't hear. Olsen winked at me, and then blocked her exit, steering her back into the room with a caustic remark. He shut the door behind her, dampening the volume on her curses.

"You look at the dispatch log yet?" he asked.

"I can't believe you just did that."

"Here, let me," he said, taking the sheet from my hand. He scanned it, and halfway down the page pointed to something: female, picked up for suspected DUI.

I nodded toward the closed door. "Marchforth?"

"You know it."

"You set me up."

He pulled a small tape recorder from his pocket and played a brief snippet from our conversation last night outside my house.

"She wasn't convinced it was you on the tape," he said. "I just needed you to confirm."

"You used me," I said.

"Yeah," he said. "I did."

I shook my head, still in shock when Sarah Dodge stepped out from the next room down the hall. She looked as betrayed as I felt.

I strode into the chief's office, slamming his door behind me.

"You let him use me!" I shouted.

The chief was on the phone. He glared, but didn't seem surprised to see me.

"I'll call you back," he said and hung up. "Sit down, Vince."

"Chief, I've known you all my life and no matter what, I've always, *always* trusted you. I can't believe you let Olsen play me like this."

"It's not a game, Vince."

"When have you ever condoned such underhanded means? A cop shows up at my house, leads me into conversation, and secretly records it?"

"Are you denying the conversation happened?"

"No, but—"

"But what? You feel foolish? You weren't the one doing the recording this time?"

"But he—"

"I've told you this a hundred times, Vince. If you would leave the police work to us, if you would just be patient and let us do our job, these embarrassments to your ego wouldn't keep happening."

"Let you do your job? I did. I called Gord and gave him the phone number from my anonymous call. I went to the bar last night because Olsen and Gord asked me to."

"You'd have gone anyway," he said.

"You don't know that."

The chief shrugged.

"I'm not sure why you're so upset," he said. "You're going to help solve a fourteen-year-old case and clear a man's name. That's a good day's work, a real community service."

The chief spread his hands open, like some kind of pastor giving me his blessing.

"I can't believe that you, of all people, were part of this."

"Vince—" he called, but I was out the door and heading down the hall.

Amy and Sarah glared at me as I passed their room; Rowena Marchforth was in the next, her head in her hands. Steve Olsen, standing in the corridor, looked so smug I wanted to pop him as I went past. But I held my tongue and got out of there as fast as I could.

Chapter Thirty-five

Outside in the parking lot, I realized that I'd blown it. So wrapped up in my own anger, I hadn't stopped to get what I needed for work that morning—comments from Olsen and the chief. The easy way out would be to call them from my cell, but I sucked it up and went back to the security window.

"Forget something, Vince?" Gail asked. She buzzed me through.

"Yeah, I need to speak with the chief again."

"He's in a meeting. Can he call you?"

"I was just back there."

"Sorry. Things got kind of crazy after you left."

"How about Steve Olsen?"

"He's part of it and, before you ask, so is Gordon."

As she said this, Gordon and the chief came around the corner to the lobby.

"Get me a unit out there—" The chief halted when he saw me.

"Get him out of here," he said.

Gail looked at me, gave a little shrug.

"Chief, listen, I need—"

"Out!" he shouted.

Gord stepped forward and took my arm. "Not now, Vince. You've got to clear out."

He steered me toward the door.

"What's going on?"

"Rowena's talking. The dominoes are falling."

"What's that supposed to mean?"

We reached the door and Gord hit the security release. He shoved me through.

"Gord, wait—"

"If this pans out, I'll call, okay? I promise."

He shut the door behind me, and I turned to see a handful of people lined up to pay their speeding ticket.

"What are you looking at?" I shouted.

I stepped in front of them, hoping to catch something through the security window. The chief stood beside the dispatcher. I couldn't hear what he was saying, but thought it looked like, "Keep it off the air."

Outside I jogged to my Bronco, jumped inside, and turned the key so the scanner came on. I saw Gord exit the station's rear door and get into his sedan. I started my engine, thinking about following, but he zoomed out of the lot and was gone before I reacted.

Chapter Thirty-six

I was sitting in my truck trying to decide what to do next when Gina knocked on my window.

"Aren't you running a little late for deadline?" she asked.

"Aren't you?"

She snorted. "Right. Why'd the cops arrest Amy again?"

"How'd you find out?"

"Because I was there, sleeping in my truck out at the Donovans when the cops woke us up and hauled her away."

"Sheesh. How's Bella taking it?"

"Not well."

"Seems like you're about to get your wish, Gina. They're pinning the bank robbery on Amy."

"How'd . . . Was it you?" She left it hanging.

"Unfortunately it was me, although not what I intended."

"I don't care. Thank you."

"Don't thank me. Thank some lady named Rowena Marchforth."

"Rowena?" She seemed to look inward a moment, and then her eyes focused again. "She was in on it, wasn't she?"

"Apparently so. Their whole plan was to set up Earl and make it look like Amy had been killed. Then, when things quieted down, Amy was supposed to reconnect with Rowena."

"Except she never did. Ro always was a sucker. She would have followed Amy straight off a cliff. That whole group of theirs was that way."

"Now I've got to cobble a story together this morning about

166

it and find out why Gord just peeled out of here like a NASCAR driver. I'm heading back to the *Chronicle*. You coming?"

"What did you mean about Gordon?" she asked.

I shrugged. "All I know is he said something about dominoes falling, whatever that was supposed to mean."

Gina snapped her fingers. "Thanks, Vince."

She spun and jogged toward her truck.

"Gina?"

She ignored me, climbed into her cab, and spun out of there.

Chapter Thirty-seven

At the *Chronicle,* Lou's editorial meeting had already started. He frowned at me when I slid into my chair, but didn't interrupt Mort, who was talking from inside his radio cave. As in past years, Mort would hide behind the equipment for as long as Lou tolerated it after the race.

Mort told about his interview with Earl's handler, Jon Bishop, and also said he was wrapping up a story with the latest information on the search for Earl.

"Did you ever find out if Perry buys back the Superior Cup from the race winners?" I asked.

"No one would go on record, but yeah, that's what he used to do. He offered seventy-five cents on the dollar. But I guess, with the price of gold rocketing up the last couple years, the mushers were more interested in holding on to the trophy. At least that's what last year's winner told me. He said Perry just about freaked when he refused to sell the thing back."

"So Perry was out the income and the raw material."

"Is this today's story, or is it leading to something bigger?" Lou asked.

"Possibly something much bigger," I said.

"Are you planning to—"

"A moment, Lou," Holmes interrupted. He held his phone in one hand, the mouthpiece covered with his other. "Breaking news."

Lou closed his eyes. "What is it, Holmes?"

I rolled my chair over to the file cabinet where our scanner sat and bumped the volume knob. The thing had been too quiet.

"The police have arrested the snowmobile trail vandal," Holmes blurted. "Remember I tried to tell you about that pet obituary?"

"Not that again," Lou growled. His eyes were still closed, but now creases from his clenching jaw and pursed lips were ruining the patient Yoda look.

"The guy's dog was hit by a snowmobile," Holmes interjected before Lou could shut him down again. "He's been avenging his dog's death."

"Are you serious?" I said.

"Didn't Deb tell you?" Holmes asked. "She's the one who suggested I give the info to the police."

"Deb didn't mention it," I said. "And there wasn't anything on the dispatch log."

"Who do you have on the phone?" Lou asked.

"Lyle Simmons. He called to thank me for the tip."

"Mort? Vince? Which one of you can take it?"

I watched Mort shrink even lower behind his radio gear. Holmes looked crestfallen.

"Why can't Holmes write it?" I said. "He did the legwork. Besides, it sounds like my wife is involved."

Lou glared my way.

"I can help him, you know, check it over."

"I'd rather you just do it."

"I've got something else cooking."

"It better be good," Lou said. "Holmes, is Lyle sending us a news release?"

Holmes talked into the phone and then said, "Yes, I'll have it by e-mail PDQ."

"All right, you put together the story—with Vince's help.

Stick to the release. Tell Lyle he needs to include a comment from the cops."

"Right," Holmes said. "I'm on it."

"What choice do I have?" Lou growled. He reached for his mug, lifted it to his lips, but before drinking put it down in disgust. "And, Holmes, we don't get paid by the inch on this, so keep it short and sweet. Got it?"

"Absolutely."

Lou turned to me. "You didn't by any chance bring me some coffee from City Hall? I'm tired of this herbal swill."

"Sorry."

"I'm sure you are. What's your big story?"

"Amy Parsons, aka Lupine Ryder, and a local woman named Rowena Marchforth, robbed the First National Bank fourteen years ago—not Earl Parsons."

"And you know this how?" he said, raising a skeptical eyebrow.

"Rowena confessed it to me last night."

"You're taking confession now?"

"She approached me as an anonymous source." I held up a hand to stave him off. "Don't worry. I told her of your objections to that. Anyway, she told me all about how she and Amy robbed the bank, faked Amy's death, and framed Earl."

"I see. And who is this Marchforth woman?"

"She and Amy Parsons were friends. Gina confirmed that for me."

"I see, so Gina's part of this too. Does everyone know about this but me?" Lou looked around the room as if expecting everybody else to raise their hands and prove his point.

"I didn't," one of the sports guys yelled.

"Anyway, the cops found out I was meeting Rowena last night, so—"

"How did they do that?"

"Long story."

"Please tell me you aren't mixed up in this. Can't you stay out of your own stories?"

"I try, but it's a small town. Besides, the cops used me."

Lou closed his eyes and massaged his temples

"I met Rowena last night," I explained. "Afterward, the cops arrested her for a DUI. When I stopped by the shop this morning to look at the dispatch log, they just happened to parade me past her interrogation room. They did it in a way that *implied* I was working for them. They also arrested Amy last night. She was in the next room over. The cops were playing them against each other, trying to get them to squeal. I think Rowena broke."

"I see." He opened his eyes and took a deep breath. "Okay, don't tell me anything else. Just do the story. I'm going to sit over here and pretend I don't have any clue what's going on."

"Uh, there's one tiny problem," I said.

A loud snort came from behind the radio cave.

Lou put his hands in front of him in a prayer pose and said, "There are no problems, only solutions." I could have sworn I saw him wink.

"You've got two hours. Work it," he said. "If they were friends in high school, find their other friends. Find their teachers. Get over to Patrice's office—"

I slapped my forehead. I'd forgotten I was supposed to be at the Historical Society yesterday afternoon.

"—and see what you can dig up in old yearbooks. And get back on the horn with Lyle. As soon as he's finished with Holmes, he'd better earn his pay and come up with some comment on this too."

I tried Gina first. I'd seen some kind of spark when she'd mentioned Amy's little clique of friends, and now I wanted to know what exactly she'd been thinking. Of course there was no answer.

I called Erin Donovan next.

"Is Gina there?"

"No," she answered. "I suppose you heard what happened?"

"Yes, Amy was arrested again."

"Poor Bella. They came banging on the door early this morning like storm troopers. Nobody would tell us a thing. Bella has totally shut down."

"I can imagine," I said. "It's probably going to get worse for her."

"Just what she needs," Erin said. "Her mom in jail again and her dad presumed dead."

"It might get worse—the cops may have reason to think Amy caused Earl's death."

"What kind of reason?"

"Something happened this morning. I still don't know what, but I'm wondering if Amy confessed to causing Earl's disappearance."

"It would never happen."

"There was the bloody ax," I said.

"I mean she wouldn't confess," Erin said. "I know that much just in the short time I've seen her. She's not talking with anyone."

"Probably not," I said. "If Gina shows up, please tell her to call me. It's urgent."

"Will do," she said. "And, Vince, please do your best to keep reminding everyone that Bella's part of this too. I'm afraid everyone's going to forget that, and she's really just a kid."

Erin was right about that. No matter how this shook out, Bella's life was now turned upside down for a while, maybe for good.

* * *

Patrice let me in the back entrance of the Historical Society. Today she wore a small red pin on her black turtleneck. Baby steps, I thought.

I gave her a quick synopsis and told her I needed to go through old Bay High yearbooks. As usual, she had the info on a table for me within minutes. She withheld her usual biting wit, obviously as interested as I was.

Patrice reminded me to use Amy's maiden name—Holt. It took us about five minutes to find the girl's senior year edition.

"Here it is," she said, holding open the page to senior photos, her finger pointing to an angrier, plumper version of Bella. The girl's apparent rage matched her fiery hair. I glanced further down the page, looking for Rowena. On my way, my eyes stopped at someone who looked familiar. An idea formed when I saw the name. Then I moved on to find Rowena on the opposite page amid a half dozen girls with the standard 70s body-wave hairdo.

I turned to the Ps. There was Earl—long hair, scruffy teen beard, and red-checked lumberjack shirt.

I flipped through the pages, scanning the candid shots and the school clubs for a glimpse of Amy, Rowena, and Earl together. I found them in a small group of about a dozen kids underneath the title *Off-road Explorers*. Amy stood front and center, and even in the faded black-and-white she radiated fury.

Rowena and Earl stood next to each other, about a half step behind Amy, smirks on their faces, like they'd just heard a bawdy joke. Behind Rowena, a geeky boy with large round glasses was trying to squeeze between the two. He had a possessive hand on Rowena's shoulder and a grimace that was probably supposed to be a smile.

I checked the list of names to be sure he was who I thought he was.

Chapter Thirty-eight

On my way out of the Historical Society I called Gina again. No answer. I checked in with Mort to see if they'd heard what the cops had going.

"Nada. You'd better get back here soon," he added. "When Lou blows, I don't want to be the only target."

"Keep your head below the electronics and you'll be safe," I said.

I hung up before he could retort, dialed Gord's cell, and left a message to call me ASAP. Then I called the cop shop to see if Gail could raise him.

"He hasn't been back since you left this morning," she said. "Same with the chief."

"Gail, please tell one of them to call me. I have info for them and it's urgent."

She promised to pass along my message, but I didn't plan to hold my breath.

A glance at my watch told me I had more than an hour; time enough to see the person once known as Twitch. I jogged out of the alley and toward Iverson's Gold Rush.

The goofy guy in the yearbook, the guy with eyes for Rowena, was Perry Iverson. He had to be the same person Gina had called Twitch. And that means he knew who stole the cup. There's no way he'd not recognize one of this two best friends from high school.

Iverson's shop was closed. No lights were on and the back door was locked.

174

I ran to the *Chronicle,* but instead of heading inside, I went to my Bronco and pulled out the phone book I kept under the seat. Perry lived on the north edge of town—a ten-minute trip.

My cell rang. It was the *Chronicle.*

"Yeah."

"Where are you, Vince?" I heard the panic in Mort's voice.

"Still chasing something down. Any news from the cops?"

"Zip. You need to get in here, man. Lou's started some kind of Gregorian chanting. It's freaking me out."

"Listen, this is going to be tight. I need to give you the back story over the phone and have you write it. I may not be back in time."

"No way, uh-uh, not going to happen."

"Don't worry, you get the byline. Ready?"

"I'm hanging up now," he said.

"Put on Holmes."

He didn't say anything, but I heard the line transfer, and Holmes came on as I pulled out of the *Chronicle*'s lot.

"Holmes, did you finish your story?"

"I'm pretty close," he said. "There's just—"

"Good. I need help with another. Can you type while I talk?"

"I *do* take obits."

"Right. Then here's what I know."

I told him about my call from Rowena, how the cops traced the number. What she said. That she was in custody. How Olsen set me up.

Holmes was good. I could hear his keyboard clacking in the background. He didn't interrupt or have me repeat anything.

I told him about Perry Iverson. For the first time he paused.

"Makes sense," he said.

"Listen, write it the best you can, but leave it open-ended. I'm still chasing something."

"What?"

"Perry. I want to talk with him. I'll call before deadline. If Lou gets antsy, give him another dose of chamomile."

"Really?"

"It's a joke, Holmes. Call you in a few."

It took me another five minutes to get to Perry's road. I slowed, looking for the street number, but it wasn't necessary: dead center in the driveway was a sky blue pickup truck.

The house was a weathered, wood-sided bungalow with a roofed porch across the front and snowdrifts on the roof. Some-one had plowed the front yard, pushing snow into huge piles off to the cabin's left. The porch deck sagged under the weight of stacked firewood.

Chapter Thirty-nine

I parked beside Gina's truck and was halfway to the porch when my phone sang out Gina's ringtone.

"Why didn't you tell me?" I asked. I continued toward the porch.

"Turn around and go back to the *Chronicle,*" she said. "Or go home. Just get away from here."

"I want to talk with Perry," I said. I saw movement in the cabin's picture window, but couldn't see through the glare.

"I'm serious, Vince. Scram!"

I stepped onto the porch. The roof cut the glare and I saw Gina watching me through the glass. Still wearing her purple parka, she held the phone to her ear with her left hand. In her right, she held a gun.

I stopped.

"C'mon, Gina."

A blur came from her left side, someone was hitting her, and they went down. The gun popped and I saw a spider web form in the window's upper corner around a hole. I grabbed the front door's handle and pushed inside.

Gina sat on the floor, holding her left shoulder. Crouching and pointing the gun my way was a guy in tan canvas overalls and a plaid shirt.

"You should have listened to her," he said. He stood, still keeping the barrel trained on me.

I scanned the room. Perry twitched away on a threadbare, green couch. A lamp lay on the floor past the couch, apparently knocked over in the scuffle. Behind that, a potbellied wood stove stuck out from the wall, its vent pipe elbowing back into a bricked-up chimney. The walls were dark wood, chinked with concrete.

The man with the gun stood up slowly. He was wiry, about my height. His face was leathery, weathered, and his hair crew cut. I saw the similarity to his high school photo.

"Earl?" I asked.

"Jeez," he said. "This is getting worse by the minute. Why are you such an idiot, Twitch?"

"It's not my fault," Perry whined.

"It sure is," Earl said, his voice rising. "If you'd just done what I said, you'd have the real cup back, Amy'd be in jail, you might finally have a shot at Ro, and I'd be free. But no, you had to give me a stupid fake and then make it worse by telling the cops it was a fake. You're dumber than you used to be."

"Bu-but I thought you were dead," Perry whined. "Anyway, I never made a real one."

"You haven't made a real cup the last couple of years, have you?" I guessed.

I caught Perry's eyes for the briefest moment as they bounced around the room. It was long enough to see I'd guessed right.

"I needed the insurance money to keep me afloat," Perry mumbled.

"What were you going to do when gold topped out and a musher tried to sell the trophy to a different jeweler?" I asked. "It was only a matter of time."

Perry acted like he hadn't heard me. I turned to Earl.

"How did it work?" I asked. "Did you cut Amy's dogs free at the start, and then in the chaos, you planted the cup and the ax in her bag?"

He kept an eye on me while he waved the gun at Gina.

"Get over there with Twitch," he told her.

"Or what?" she said. "You aren't going to shoot me, Earl."

Gina stood, still rubbing her shoulder. I thought about Gina's truck at Lake Margaret.

"Were you helping him all along, Gina? Did you pick him up at Lake Margaret after he made it look like he'd had an accident?"

"Are you nuts?" she said. "I didn't know anything about this until you told me about Rowena."

When she said the name, it all came together. Something about Rowena's coat had struck me at the bar last night and now I knew why. I'd seen her at Lake Margaret—the loner Ari had called to. She must have been there to pick up Earl after he ditched his sled and his dogs.

And that's why Earl hadn't run with his regular lead dog. Teej had said something about that. Earl planned to disappear, and that meant giving up his team, but like any musher, he just couldn't part with his favorite dog.

"You had it made," I said. "Everyone thought you were dead. You could have walked away."

"Amy would have walked too," Earl said. "'Cause of that idiot."

Earl waved the gun toward Perry and the man threw up his arms as if they'd protect him from a bullet.

"It's your fault," Perry whined. "If you'd let me in on the whole plan, if I'd known you weren't dead, then I wouldn't have told the cops about the fake."

"He has a point," Gina said.

"Shut up," Earl growled.

"Rowena told the cops everything this morning," I said. "They'll be here as soon as they figure out you're no longer at her place."

"Gina already gave me that wonderful news," he said. He turned toward her. "Give me your keys."

"Not until we seal the deal," she said.

"What deal?" I asked.

"He disappears, forever," she said. "No claims to Bella."

"Did you even know you had a daughter?" I asked.

"I ain't stupid," he growled. "I figured it out once I put two and two together and realized Amy was Lupine Ryder."

"How long ago was that?" I asked.

"A few years back," he said. "I'd heard other mushers talking about her and I just had a feeling. Then I saw her at a race and knew right away. She changed her hair and got skinny, but that's about all she changed—except maybe she got even meaner."

"You can't just walk away from Bella," I said. "She's your daughter."

"Mind your own business, Vince," Gina said.

"Walking away is the best thing I could do," Earl said. "Bella's spent the last fourteen years being warped by Amy. Ain't no way she'd have anything to do with me. Besides, I've been alone with my dogs too long. Kind of prefer their company."

"But what about clearing your name? Doesn't that mean anything?"

"Nope. What's the point? I'll never get back those years."

I started to argue, but Gina cut me off. "Vince, just shut up." She reached into her coat pocket and Earl stiffened.

"Relax, Earl," she said. "I'm just getting you the keys."

"Where can you possibly go?" I asked.

"To die, of course," Earl said. Gina tossed him the keys and he caught them in his free hand. "That's what I set out to do in the first place. Now get out of my way. I won't kill you, but I don't have a problem shooting you somewhere painful if you try to stop me."

I put my hands up and moved toward the couch, near Perry. Earl sidestepped over to the door, took one look at Gina, and then turned and ran toward her truck. I heard the engine fire up and then whine as he backed out.

As soon as I was sure he was gone, I flipped open my cell phone. Gina grabbed my wrist before I could dial.

"No, Vince."

She held my wrist firmly, but not so hard I couldn't break free.

"Let him go . . . ," she said. "It may be my only chance with Bella."

My phone rang with Lou's tone. I twisted my hand free and stared at Gina a moment longer, and then I pressed the silence button.

Chapter Forty

I took another of my mother's cookies from the tin on the chief's desk and checked my watch for about the twentieth time: one o'clock. I picked up the photo frame, a recent addition to the usually bare surface, and checked out my daughter, wrapped in Mom's arms, their mischievous matching grins making you wonder what they'd been up to.

The photo made me realize Gina had missed out on that with her granddaughter. She'd never get to share those childhood years. Was it fair to deprive my mother of the same by moving? Should we be obligated to stay in Apostle Bay?

The chief banged through the door and saved me from stewing over it more.

"Gina's truck went off the road and crashed into Superior about ten miles north of town," he said.

He walked behind his desk, set my phone on the desktop next to his landline, and then sat. The cops had confiscated my phone when they arrived at Perry's house—as evidence, they claimed, but I knew it was to keep me from calling the *Chronicle*.

"You think we'll find Earl's body?" he asked.

I shrugged. I wasn't in a helpful mood. "Maybe Olsen has a new place to fish for a while," I said.

"Yeah, maybe."

"Can I go now? I'd like to get in touch with Deb. And Lou. He's probably fired me twice by now for not calling in."

"Look, Vince, I know you tried to reach us. I appreciate that."

182

I shrugged again. Being right for once didn't feel as good as I'd thought it would.

"And you did the right thing telling us about the anonymous call."

"Too bad you guys didn't reciprocate."

"I'm sorry about that. I shouldn't have let Olsen pull that stunt."

"You're right." I stood. "Can I go?"

"Maybe I'm getting too old for this job," he said, more to himself than to me. He pushed my cell phone toward me. "Sure, Vince. Just one more thing. You know we arrested Arne Everson for the snowmobile vandalism."

"I heard you had a suspect. Some guy whose dog had been run over."

"That's right. He confessed. I'm sorry Deb took the heat about that. It wasn't right."

"Nope, it wasn't."

"What's going to happen to Bella?" I asked.

"She's going to stay with the Donovans for now. The rest depends on what happens with Amy."

"Will Gina get to see her?"

The chief shrugged. "That's up to the judge. They do try to keep families together, so it's probable."

The chief stood. He looked like he wanted to shake hands or something, but he grabbed the tin and handed it to me.

"Deb and Glory are waiting for you in the lobby. Why don't you give these to the little munchkin on your way out?"

"Sure, Chief," I said.

I took the cookies from him and started toward the door.

"Vince," he said. "You forgot your phone."

He held it toward me.

"No, I didn't forget it, Chief," I said. "I'll leave it with you for a few more days."

Then I headed for my wife and daughter.

Epilogue

The police search and rescue team never found Earl Parsons' body. His death was ruled an accident, caused by slippery roads. Parsons' handler, Jon Bishop, inherited all of the musher's possessions, including his kennel and home in Minnesota. The FBI searched his property and could find no evidence that Parsons had preplanned a disappearance, despite Steve Olsen's belief otherwise.

According to Bishop, Parsons' lead dog, Polaris, and a litter of pups he'd sired, escaped from his kennel soon after Bishop returned to Minnesota. The dogs were never found.

Police Chief Dale Weathers announced his retirement in June after some forty years on the force. He and Mom were able to tolerate each other on a weeklong Caribbean cruise, so they decided to try a little longer vacation. They've rented a condo in Arizona for three months next winter.

The Apostle Bay City Commission has chosen Gordon Greenleaf as the city's new chief. Archie Freeman resigned in protest.

Amy Parsons and Rowena Marchforth were both convicted of armed robbery at the First National Bank. They are currently serving their sentences in a federal penitentiary.

Perry Iverson awaits trial on embezzlement charges and faces up to ten years in prison if convicted. Iverson's Gold Rush is bankrupt. The Superior Challenge sled dog committee has tracked down past winners of the race and replaced any awards that were not real gold. The Elk Ridge Hunt and Fish Club decided to give a cash prize at next year's event.

Thomas Holmes, aka Dr. Death, turned down Lou's offer of promotion to reporter. He still works part-time writing obituaries for the *Chronicle* and has started a pet memorial website.

The police received an anonymous tip that the snowmobiler who hit and killed Arne Everson's dog on the city's bike path was Jack Reynolds. Upon investigation they found hair and blood samples stuck to the side of Reynolds' snow machine that matched the DNA of Everson's dog. Prosecutor Lyle Simmons said there was no crime committed, but Everson, who was sentenced to five hundred hours of community service maintaining bike paths and snowmobile trails, is suing the former Apostle Bay mayor.

Bella Ryder continues to live with Erin and Teej Donovan and will attend Bay High in the fall. Gina Holt visits her daily and their relationship is beginning to thaw.

At work, Gina has been sharing plans for a kennel she hopes to build if Bella moves in with her. And she recently gave Bella a male sled dog pup—just in case her granddaughter wants to try her hand at breeding. What Gina hasn't told anyone but me is that she found the pup in a small kennel on her porch one morning. The attached note said *Little Dipper.*

This summer we started building an addition to our home. We're adding an office where Deb can study and work on her PhD in education. She's taking a leave of absence from Bay

High and has enrolled in a Michigan State program where she can do most of the coursework in Apostle Bay.

When she completes the program, we'll go where the work takes us. In the meantime, the new construction will also include a master bedroom and conversion of our old room into a nursery.

Deb is pregnant and the sonogram shows I'll now have three women keeping me in line.

Glory has said she can't wait to teach her new sister how to eat humongous sticky buns.